# CATALYST in PALM BEACH

By Casey Tennyson

Catalyst in Palm Beach ignites Awareness through a tale of travels, trysts, tragedies, universal Truths and the quest for unrequited True Love.

INSIDE: The quest for an eternal twin soul sparks a suspenseful epic life era. Intriguing twists strip the superficial to reveal the essence of integrity and Truth. The main character Cat dances with distractions and illusions as they melt away to reveal a life purpose. Adventure travels take Cat around the world. The spiritual journey brings her home to embrace the tender parts of humanity.

AUTHOR: Casey Tennyson has used her writing as a leader in advertising, marketing, publishing and ghostwriting. Her fifth book "Catalyst in Palm Beach" sets the stage for sequels. Many of her books are based in Florida and the Caribbean where she finds her creative energy and inspiration. Tennyson also is the publisher of Chart charity art magazine in Florida.

Copyright 2019, Cutting Edge Communications, Inc.
All rights reserved. No part of this book may be produced or stored in any form whatsoever without the prior written consent of the publisher and copyright holder. Reviews may quote brief passages without written consent of the publisher as long as proper credit is given.

Title:
Catalyst in Palm Beach

Published in the USA by:
Cutting Edge Communications, Inc.

Written by:
Casey Tennyson

International Standard Book Number
ISBN number 978-0-9855264-3-6

OTHER BOOKS BY CASEY TENNYSON
Available to order from Amazon.com, other online sources and select retailers

CLEVER "'**Secrets of the Southern Shells**' is a very clever and original allegory containing much wisdom that has been passed down from Southern mothers to their daughters, the Southern Belles. This charming book, filled with very attractive marine artwork, relates a powerful story of sea creatures, and how one, a mere starfish, overcomes impossible obstacles and achieves her dreams because she faithfully heeds her mother's timeless advice. In seven words: Buy it, read it, and gift it!" – Bill Guggenheim, co-author of bestseller "Hello From Heaven!"

WORLD NEEDS TO READ "I loved the book '**Marlins Cry A Phishing Story**.' The world needs to read it. I loved the author's description of fishing. Her observations of people on the docks in the Bahamas is better than any focus group. Her observations of life hit home, like when she described the boat owner seen for the first time in a weakened state brought to tears, or when she noted that when it's your problem it seems bigger up close even though solvable from afar. The book hit me between the eyes." – Scott L. Richardson, Attorney at Law

INSPIRATIONAL "I truly enjoyed reading '**Marlins Cry A Phishing Story**.' My very favorite line in the book is 'You have the protection of the wings of one thousand angels. Look up. Protecting them are one thousand more for every star of the sky.' Thank you for a very compelling, yet a bit scary, read. And thank you for that line of inspiration when some days life seems a bit too much to handle. LOVED IT." – Tracie Sayyah

BIG BOOK OF LIFE "'**Marlins Cry A Phishing Story**' is more than a slice of life. In a few succinct chapters this is a Big Book of Life. Each chapter has a novel-size volume of depth. The way the author creates a sequence of words of profound simple truths of humanity makes her a powerful, relevant voice of our time. The book reads as if you were in all the places, you were involved in the dramas, you were part of the scene and part of the very same life. What a voice for modern story telling weaving moments in time ... how words have power to express universal truths. The main character asks, 'What do you stand for and how do you live up to it?' Everyone knows the sharks, the alligators, characters but to understand the Marlin is big. I am going to read this book time and again for deeper meaning. I am an avid reader, and when I read this book, I thought 'This is a writer. Casey Tennyson can write.'" - Xenia Psihas

CONTENTS



CHAPTERS

**Seek Truth through LENS**.
Dwell upon that which is
Lovely,
Enlightened,
Noble,
Serene.

## INTRODUCTION by the Author

I started this book in March 2015. I wrote in Florida and the Bahamas. The manuscript sat idle for several years as duties and distractions delayed the completion. I edited the manuscript and wrote the last chapter for the book in September 2019 on Labor Day weekend.

Ironically, that weekend Cat 5 Hurricane Dorian devastated many of the Bahamian settings of my previous books such as Abaco and Grand Bahama Island. The catastrophic current news added an eerie surreal backdrop to the ultimate message of this book, which manifested itself as an urging for Americans to refocus on basic core values within ourselves and also in our society. As I proofed the delayed manuscript, I realized other island settings in this book likewise were wiped out by hurricanes since I started writing, such as St. Barths, and Little Palm Island on Little Torch Key and Cheeca Lodge in Islamorada both in The Keys.

The material world is fleeting. The crux is the soul not the soil of a society. Things don't last. Change is inevitable. There are no coincidences. So, we ask ... What do we treasure? What if we lost all monetary and material possessions? What do you cherish in your heart? For the time we have here, what do we value and what should we do? What is eternal?

The book offers a strong notion to listen to our inner selves and realize that this is where our treasure lies. Our treasure is not of the world, but in our hearts. I used primarily older examples of a spiritual journey for a few reasons. First of all, you don't know where you are going until you know where you have been. There are more recent and more profound examples and perhaps will be shared at a later time. To reveal a spiritual experience makes one feel more vulnerable than sharing a physical nakedness. It reveals the intrinsic nature of ones inner self.

I layered the spiritual experiences with fiction to carry the story line.

The book is intended to be entertaining and also enlighten spiritual growth ideas for readers. The book gives permission to explore our Constitutional Right for Freedom of Religion and our God-given right to seek spirituality as a way to experience personally the Living Spirit in all of us.

The book went to the publishing house on 9/11/19 at 11:11 a.m.

# CHAPTER 1
# RAISING THE BAR

"Starting a film, are you Charlotte?" Donna asked, as she lit white vanilla tea candles. She dimmed the lamps in her living room not far from my home in Winter Park, Fla.

It was December 2002 and chilly enough for light sweaters at our biweekly noon meeting. We met for about a year after 9/11. I met her when my advertising agency pitched an executive team of a startup technology company. This was one of our last meetings before she took another executive job in another market. I wasn't seeking the esoteric or occult or enlightened disciplines. I was, however, eagerly and earnestly seeking explanations for significant spiritual experiences and occurrences in my own life. Teachers, mentors and confidants appeared though the years to guide me. Donna was one.

"It's called 'Raising the Bar.' It's a documentary about the bar scene and how singles mingle there to find love in the most unlikely place of all to find love. I wore a psychic costume for a Halloween party this year. Presenting my pink crystal ball toy, I asked people, 'What would you like to ask my crystal ball?' Men asked, 'Will I get laid tonight?' Women asked, 'Will I meet my soul mate tonight?' They aren't looking for each other," I gave my elevator speech.

She took a few deep breaths, and closed her bon bon brown eyes. We settled into our comfortable chairs, and she started her reading, "Your clever lines will become inspirational, not motivational. Simple. To-the-point. Zen-ism. Black-and-white. Different. This film is about the American Dream. Your work is the American Dream and your romantic life will converge as you do your work. You will experience a love unlike any other. But it's not what you imagine it to be."

Today was the end of 2015. I was dreaming of 2002. It was that time of morning when still in dream state as you awaken, and you pull subconscious reality into the physical world. Living spiritually in the physical world is much like snorkeling. At first the mask and fins feel awkward. As you submerge, you discover a hidden unfamiliar world beneath the water's surface. As you practice, you effortlessly maneuver your buoyant body between the water and air, sensing both at once. Living in two worlds of reality is much like floating in the ocean.

My guidance for the day, and for my life purpose, is what one thinks about on New Year's Eve. My dream state partial-answer was from an intuitive reading played back in Technicolor in my mind as if I was reliving the message. Anticipating one's life's purpose has made it pleasurable through the years to enjoy the process. I certainly knew when it was not my moment of purpose. During the down time, I would keep my writing skills and promotional skills sharp so when I was called upon for my life mission, I would be prepared. I had lived a rich and blessed life of adventure so far, waiting for the time of knowing to fulfill my purpose. The marketing person in me looked at this meantime phase as an opportunity for marketing research. Donna said my target for my books and films would be my own peer group of what she described as yuppie, social, party-types and creative people. I would later intuitively be led to a second group, the nation's wealthiest.

# CHAPTER 2
# IT'S A PIRATE'S LIFE FOR ME

I woke by myself in a tousled bed. I didn't remember Tennis Player leaving. My snug Palm Beach Island guesthouse cradled me in luxe bliss. Joy seeped into the cozy apartment through the wood blinds with the first hint of sunlight. A ray caught a crystal by the window and sprayed a rainbow across the white stucco wall spilling onto the oak floor. I adorned my morning uniform, a two-piece swimsuit, white cotton beach cover and turquoise flip flops with a gold starfish charm. I brushed my hair into a blonde straight foot-long ponytail. I took two aspirin with a Starbucks coffee cooler I had placed in the refrigerator the day prior.

"Be prepared and practice what you beach," I smiled to myself. I tended to let the hair in that ponytail down when I was at the beach. In part, that is the intended use of a beach place.

I used the weekend beach getaway as a writer's retreat. I didn't have television or other distractions in the guesthouse, well, except an occasional house guest. I hung paintings of fish and beach scenes that I painted when I was between writing projects. I was always creating. A small portable radio played "Tainted Love" by Soft Cell from the 1980s, "The love we share seems to go nowhere, and I've lost my light, for I toss and turn, I can't sleep at night ..."

In my portable plastic files of binders, I found the journal notes I made around 9/11 and placed them on the counter to read later, based on the directive from my pre-dawn dream about that time period.

In my last book, readers remembered and commented on the chapter that had a steamy shower scene. They, ok not readers, but guys told me to start my next book with a sensuous scene. I found it awkward and uncomfortable to write the first one. I decided to pen some notes about last evening while it was pressed fresh in my mind. I wrote, "Animal sounds. Wild cats. Primal. Uninhibited." I didn't have much of a vocabulary for sex scenes.

I checked my e-mail and texts from my iPhone tucked inside a teal and lime green starfish cover. I posted a New Year's message on social media a few lines from "Ring Out Wild Bells" by Alfred Lord Tennyson, an uncle from five generations back on my father's side, "... Ring in the love of truth and right, Ring in the common love of good ..."

I tossed the iPhone in my packed trusty pirate pack, a Jansport black backpack printed with pink hearts and pirate skull-and-crossbones. The backpack had carried my personal treasures around the world with me on numerous adventures and explorations. I spritzed aerosol sunscreen on my British-heritage lily-white skin. I headed out for my morning beach walk. I left the radio playing "Keep Your Head Up" by Andy Grammer, "Only rainbows after rain, the sun will always come again, it's a circle, circling, around again ..."

The balmy 70 degree thick salt air bathed me in an oxygen skin-hug as I cracked my door open. I put on my Chanel classic black sunglasses to cloak the startling light. A meaty 10 inch curly tail lizard stood sentry basking in the sun on the second stair from the bottom. He darted into the confederate jasmine climbing up the stair rail. He waited till I dropped within one stair of him, as always. The banister knob at the bottom of the staircase was loose, just like on "It's a Wonderful Life." Just like George Bailey, I had a decent life, but not yet wonderful. I longed for wonderful. I defined wonderful as being a family with my twin soul.

The knob had been nailed back, but not repainted. The house could use pressure washing, gardening and chlorine in the fountain. It's like collecting jars full of shells on your first few beach walks, then walking past shells on subsequent walks. Or after you fill a closet of Gucci and Prada purses, you don't care for them as tenderly as the first one. Owning numerous houses in one of the richest zip code in the world must be quite the same. I rent. The beauty of renting is you overlook the imperfections. In Realtor words, "Location. Location. Location." The location was perfect for me, so I renewed the lease over and over again, between bouts of shopping for condos on the island and bungalows over the bridges in much more affordable West Palm Beach.

I walked past a block of mixed Colonial, Georgian, Mediterranean and Contemporary houses. The luxury winter resort island was in high season and high spirits. The homes wore twinkling lights and lush glittering décor. A pair of feral cats darted from the sidewalk behind the 12 foot high ficus hedge. The grey duo hissed at me with arched backs. Their tiny alert eyes glared suspiciously as I passed. The cameras watched me, too. The island was full of wild cats and lots and lots of cameras.

The clock tower at Worth Avenue read 8-o-clock. The leer jets streamed overhead down the beach to the south of the island over Donald Trump's Mar-a-lago to the executive airport off Southern

Boulevard. Fridays displayed a parade of airborne testosterone toys, as did a holiday such as now.

I walked down the weathered wood stairs at the southernmost access to the public beach. The word "Hope" was carved into the railing.

I walked along the water's edge at high tide along a line of shore-bound seaweed. I watched my pedicured pink toes sink into the wet grains, scraping the polish off the tips.

"Preoccupation with seaweed and shells prevents sensing the wonderment of the whole. Sense your surroundings," my inner voice spoke to me.

I moved a few feet to the drier sand with less sharp shells, and stood for a moment in awe of the horizon. Paradise glowed before me.

The sea looked as a Caribbean shore. The same turquoise and aqua waters flow from the islands off Florida. The Gulf Stream comes closest to the United States in Palm Beach bringing the sea life with the currents. A school of flamboyant spinner sharks thrust themselves into the air 30 feet offshore. The splashes were the only audible sounds as the waves were lapping on the shore in lake-like tranquility.

My own footprints crunched the top layer of virgin sugar sand encrusted by the last rain. Only a few seagulls left tracks before me as they took flight from my path as I strolled along. I grabbed my camera to capture the athletic seaside X-Games. While the spinner's antics screamed, "watch me," gravity yanked them out of view each time before the lens clicked.

"You cannot tame what is wild," Y spoke to me in my inner voice. I could hear my spiritual guidance clearly on the Palm Beach shore. Observing nature was one way I would get messages to start and guide my day.

I renamed Y from V for inner-voice in 2014 when I asked my spiritual advisor Molly the name of my spirit guide. We all have a name for our spiritual relationships, such as Spirit, Universe, angels, fairies, inner voice, but for me it is God. Molly said He is always with me and in constant contact with me. "He identified himself in an ancient language. I cannot pronounce his name, but it begins with a Y. You both have been in this world since ancient times," she had explained to me. I trusted Y, and thus, had experienced a purposeful, albeit, very imperfect life to date. I had made many mistakes.

The topic of my meditation of the morning was Ted, the bad-boy boyfriend. Y's advice was generally poetic, concise, and most always accurate. The answer sometimes was a question, sometimes a riddle. Many times, I would have to ask further questions to fully understand His meaning. I didn't ask more. I didn't really want to know about "wild." A vision of Ted and Captain Ed après ski at Little Nell surrounded by fur-clad, diamond studded ski bunnies in my mind popped on the horizon like a movie screen.

"Good morning Cat Sunshine," beamed J as he broke my meditation.

The Ted vision melted like an Aspen snowflake from my consciousness.

# CHAPTER 3
# J WALKING

Where Y left off, J picked up. He was a singer-songwriter one-hit wonder from the 1970s who had rented in Palm Beach on and off for decades. He lived a modest life to afford and perpetuate his beach lifestyle. His name was long and hyphenated, something like James Henry Milton Something-or-other the Fourth. I called him J. His slender tan tone physique silhouetted against the blaring reflection of the vast white beach. Men like J after several generations in Palm Beach tend to have narrow shoulders and hips inherited from petite model-like size-zero mothers. They also inherit gorgeous faces like J's. What they don't inherit, plastic surgeons fix with fillers, facelifts, tummy tucks and hair plugs. He kept a baseball hat to cover his bald spot and dark blonde curls spilled down his neck to his shoulders. The baseball hats all had logos of 1970s bands he had played with as an opening act or as an extra in their bands. He hopped over the white scallop-topped sorbet-colored concrete wall by the Worth Avenue public beach to join me. We turned and walked south from the lifeguard beach to the residential beach towards Billionaire Row. J was highly educated and well-read in the arts and humanities. His philosophy and history interests intrigued me. They were go-to topics for stealth subject change when he would attack Ted.

"Life is good?" he inquired.

"Yes! Life is always good as a writer. Chaos is for content and calm is for documenting the chaos," I responded.

"So, why solo?" he inquired smugly.

"If you are asking about Ted, he's in Aspen," I responded with an unintentional sigh.

"If you don't tie your yacht to your dock, it floats away, you know," he advised bending his head down and looking at me over his Ray Bans.

"Ted's with Owen's boat captain for their annual guy ski trip," I added the detail like it would make the remark more palatable.

"The Ted and Ed show appearing now on the Aspen slopes! Shouldn't Ed be at sea level on Blue Daze, not at 8,000 foot elevation?" he sneered and shook his head.

I would almost assume J had a schoolboy crush on me the way he chided Ted, except he never asked me on a date. He was my beach buddy. I hadn't ruled out that he was gay. Maybe Ted hired him as a spy. Ted had hired spies and bodyguards to watch me during a dicey period in unlucky 2013 for my protection. J's intentions didn't matter. J was not my mystery. Ted was my mystery of the day.

"Blue Daze is docked here in Palm Beach at Brazilian Dock. Ed would love to be reeling in mahi and island hopping. Actually, I've been taking care of the boat the last few months. Owen isn't himself. He's not using his boat, which is the first clue. He told me I can use the New York apartment, too. He's overseas for months at a stretch. He's paying my monthly public relations fees, but he's given me minimal projects. I assume he's generating a new client and at any time now, my ad agency will be very busy! Owen was in process of retiring, now he's more active than ever, in a very quiet way," I successfully changed the subject to my client.

In sheepdog fashion, J nudged me to flatter sand on the sloping beach. He insisted walking on the flat area was better for posture and back alignment.

J circled back to the man topic, "So, speaking of quiet, you are keeping mum. I noticed a blue convertible in your parking space last night that wasn't your color. The Tennis Player perhaps?"

"I already told you my next man has to have a last name beginning with M. My initials when I married became 'CATS' and I intend for my next four marriages to spell 'MEOW' so my epitaph will be 'CATS MEOW,'" I grinned.

"Your words are silly but your heart is serious. You can't continue to be a runaway bride and also have your heart's desire," he advised like a logical college professor.

"You have a very strong personality, a born leader. You push men to the edge, just to see how they will react. Then you push them over, just for curiosity, not to be mean. You are surrounded by men. They are like flowers to you. You like to see how they smell. You need time to yourself. Writing is a lonely profession. You find you are happy by yourself. But your longing for love lingers. You find peace around the water, you like boating, sailing, travel, and romance. Find a man who enjoys the same things and quit being afraid to commit," he took a Palm-Beach-pause as a private jet screamed overhead.

"You don't like committing in relationships because you are so deeply affected when it ends. It affects everyone but it takes you so long to heal. You have to understand that all things have a beginning and an end. Just like a plant. It's natural that it ended. Just because it ends, doesn't mean it was bad. It wasn't supposed to last. Your relationships didn't fail, they ended. You picked your husband and children before you were ever born for spiritual reasons," he was reading me. I could always tell because behind his Ray Bans, his eyes would close into little slits as he listened to his own inner voice.

"You attract successful men who are accustomed to controlling their surroundings," he continued his psychic profile, "So they control you, too. Then you rebel. Hello Tennis Player! Charlotte, he's your rebellion and it's OK. Ted is dating others," he jabbed.

"I'm not positive Ted is dating. We have a long-distance relationship. We defined ourselves as exclusive initially. We talked about marriage early on and that discussion fizzled. We tell each other we love each other. He assures me I'm the only one. We call each other boyfriend and girlfriend, some ten years now. We've never fully committed because we don't fully complete each other. He is my best friend. He is my travel companion. We both have flexible schedules and can work anywhere in the world, and we do! I'll be with him in Aspen for spring skiing. We're leaving for Costa Rica and the Keys this week. We boat and fish and ski and adventure all over the world. I don't have anyone else in my life that can travel with me. First of all, most people don't have time and / or the funds. Secondly, we are compatible. We travel well together," I explained.

"And, please, I wouldn't call what I do with Tennis Player dating. It's playing. He's too young for me to date him," I spilled.

"There is no too young in Palm Beach. If anything, you've been the one that is too young a few times. What about the mature men you've dated here. Ring up a few of those to ring in your new year," J suggested.

"When I was 40 and dated 60-year-olds, it was different. I wanted a playmate. Now I want someone my own age to grow old together," I pondered.

"Some of the mature men I dated previously are still smoking hot, so I wouldn't rule out all men-of-experience," I countered myself in yen-yang indecisiveness.

"I still on occasion see King Midas when he visits the island. Everything that man touches turns to gold. As he gets older, he dates younger though. He still wants a 40-year-old me," I said.

A blue convertible beeped from South Ocean Boulevard over the looming 20-foot-high concrete sea wall protecting the mansions. A chiseled-faced strikingly handsome brunette tan 30-something waved at us.

"Now there's a hot number!" blurted J.

"He is a ten," I confided with a grin.

"But he's young in the bad way. Instead of spending New Year's with me, he is with his boys at Cucina. I'll be three blocks away with the grownups at the new The Steak Out with Ann. Want to join us? I've spent New Year's in my single life sometimes with dates and sometimes with friends in all sorts of random places. I've been in Paris, London, Santa Monica, North Conway in New Hampshire, The Bahamas, Naples, Winter Park where I live, of course. New York is on my list. I frequent the City but haven't seen the ball drop yet in Time Square. This year Ann wanted to come to Palm Beach. I wish she would visit more, but she stays in the Mayberry of Florida, Winter Park," I said.

We trekked in the thick sand by the guesthouses, studios, cabanas, and decks on the ocean side of the Ocean Boulevard that belong to the mansions across the street. J scoured piles of beached seaweed and sorted through bits of flotsam and jetsam on the semi-private stretch of virtually unoccupied beach.

"What do you do with all that driftwood, sea glass, shells and debris?" I inquired.

"I make garden art. You've seen my creations. I send them home with friends then make more," he replied.

Several hundred seagulls huddled together all facing the morning sun. They looked like manufactured stuffed animals all off the same assembly line. They all stood about 10 inch tall with fluffy grey wings, white breasts, black beaks, white dots on their black tails, black feet, all chirping the same birdie song. They pattered a few feet as we passed them keeping a safe 10 foot distance from us.

"What do you see?" I asked J.

"Birds," he replied.

"So, if I wasn't here talking to you, I would be paying attention to nature. Because we are all connected, I can get guidance for my day through nature. Birds are particularly communicative. Maybe because they can easily travel to wherever you might be and through motion and sound can convey a message," I said.

"Some parrots named Polly ask for crackers. I'm not sure about seagulls," he mocked.

"They don't actually speak, of course. You and I might get entirely different messages because we are unique people with different agendas for our day. For example, what I zone in on is the single extra-large dark grey seagull. He is trying to blend. He's twice as tall and has a big orange beak. He's pruning himself, his head tucking under his wings, trying to conceal his presence. If you look at breeding in nature, dark will take over light. So, that tells me to be aware of who is around me who might be on the dark side," I said.

A pod of dolphins bobbed by in the crystal-clear water near the shore close enough we could hear the release of air from their blow holes.

"Eleven," I counted, "Eleven is the sign of high spirituality. I notice 11:11 both a.m. and p.m. on my watch each day as a reminder that I am not alone. That is another sign from the Universe about today."

"I also hear song lyrics in my soul. Some words seem louder to me and resonate with what I need to hear that day. Songs were significant to me a few years ago, before that it was art and visual cues. I can also get spiritual guidance through intercession through Y talking through another person, something I read, radio or television ... I receive spiritual messages in a number of ways," I added, not mentioning the "Tainted Love" very specific example from an hour ago.

"So, it seems if we can connect to Spirit, we could avoid mistakes and mishaps," J inquired philosophically.

"Life begs to be lived. A perfect life would bore me. You know this. You just told me five minutes ago. You just want me to entertain you with gossip and sordid details of my past ... and the 24 hours," I chuckled.

With intensified breathing from the brisk walk, J breathed, "Any regrets?"

"I regret in my teens using baby oil instead of sunscreen. I got melanoma. In my late twenties, I lost twin babies. In my thirties, I got weekly pedicures with razors used on the soles, costing me 20 dollars a week for callous remover at my spa now. In my forties, I regret being naive about cyber stalkers and con guys," I spit out in nearly one breath.

"Quick response!" he exclaimed acting amused, adding, "Cyber stalkers and con guys? What?"

"I have put that horrific experience in my past. I can tell you sometime. Actually, you can just read my last book on the topic of the 2011 scare. There was a second 8 month long incident in the year of Unlucky 2013," I responded.

He stopped, pulled off his glasses and gave me a how-dare-you glare and scolded, "I can't believe you haven't told me this story. I'll respect your wishes to withhold for now. So, want to share any regrets in love?"

"Those that I have loved became a part of my being, it would be like asking me if I regretted having my arm," I quipped.

I continued, "For example, last month at Hannibal's in Winter Park I spotted a man across the restaurant. I pointed to him as Ann and I walked in to the piano bar and said, 'That man looks interesting to me.' After a few songs, Mr. Interesting requested 'Sweet Caroline' to Dr. Jack, who was guest singing. Local Winter Parkers join in when Michael is on the piano. Mr. Interesting then sat down next to us and led the whole bar in the chorus. He was handsome, gregarious and funny. He had dark blonde hair for sideburns and thinning hair on top. He was tall, so you'd miss the bald spot. He wore funky big glasses with conservative attire. 'Charlotte, it's me!' he exclaimed, cluing me into his identity. He was my tenth-grade boyfriend! My eyes can fail me, but my spirit was drawn to him immediately. We connected literally spiritually from across the room, then beside one another on bar stools covering 30 years of life events. He had several near-death experiences and claimed he thought about me each time as he entered the other side. That is another topic! So, the point is, the connection of love lives on. Love is forever, even if not in this lifetime," I explained.

I added in song, "Michael, Dr. Jack and others were harmonizing Frank Sinatra's 'Where and When' as I walked in that day. I remember because the song is about reincarnation, our eternal connectedness."

I sang slightly out of tune, "And so it seems that we have met before, and laughed before and loved before, but who knows where and when ..."

"Now is a part of forever. Palm Beach is the ultimate adult playground. You can flirt with men in Bentleys, boats and bars. Add one to your soulmate stash. Stash and trash. Ted has to go," he laughed.

# CHAPTER 4
# PI-LANDERS AND A FUJITIVE

"Palm Beach is a pirate's playground. The island attracts pretty boys, Peter Pans and pirates. We congregate on the island to find, hide, bury, dig up, trade, spend, and flaunt treasure. It's easy here to bury your treasure, or any secret. The social scene is comprised of mostly the self-absorbed, so it's easy to deflect any real substantive conversation. Snowbirds and seasonal tourists are floating in and out each week. Some of the famous are hiding their image and trying to fit in and be normal. Normal people are trying to create a mirage with a yearning for fame. They are Palm Beach Pirates. I call us Pi-landers, like Pi and islanders, for Pirate Islanders," I summed up dating life in Palm Beach.

"Rest assured there is no buried treasure. There are no secrets. There are only things we try not to tell. Then someone else tells them for you. Since we've been friends, you know all of my dates with Pi-landers. And I've only told you about Tennis Player. It's a small town," I continued.

"It's not just about dating. That is secondary for me. As a Palm Beach Pirate, I'm here both hiding something and finding something. It's sort of like in 'Indiana Jones and the Kingdom of the Crystal Skull,' the 2008 film with Harrison Ford, the crystal skulls didn't want real treasure, but knowledge was their treasure. My treasure is my life's purpose, something I've been actively seeking for years. I've been led to Palm Beach with many clues to fulfill my purpose. As my purpose, my treasure, is revealed, my twin soul will manifest. Purpose and person will present themselves simultaneously," I explained.

"How do you know?" he asked.

"I know that I don't know, but I believe. Believing is knowing for me," I said.

"Also, with the word pirate, the first syllable, Pi is the sixteenth letter of the Greek alphabet. It's the ancient unsolvable algorithm of the circumference of a circle at 3.145 to infiniti. Following my life purpose and my twin soul can feel equally as unsolvable," I continued.

"Speaking of pirates ..." J said, pointing to a "Blair Witch" style man-made altar of sorts in the seaweed with a backpack surrounded by freshly arranged shells.

The backpack was sealed in clear plastic wrapping. It had the same fabric design as mine except in blue. Attached to the front of the backpack was a note sealed in a sandwich bag with the name "Charlotte" scribbled in chicken scratch writing in blue ink.

"The Port Lucaya Freeport Fugitive," I blurted.

The sun darted behind a cloud casting an eerie shadow over the beach as if a warning from the Universe of our entrapment. Wide-eyed, I observed the footprints coming from the ocean, then tracking back in the water. We were a good 45 minute trek from escaping the 40 foot wide stretch of beach between the water and walls. You couldn't go up the private entrances of estates so we would have to get back to the public access beach at Worth Avenue.

"This is so creepy. First, it's creepy that a grown man would carry a backpack of this juvenile design. Secondly, creepy that it matches mine. Thirdly, it was creepy that in Port Lucaya in Freeport, Bahamas The Fugitive left this on the picnic table at the marina by Blue Daze every day during New Year's week in 2013 when I was on the boat. The other boaters all speculated about the strange man. What is creepier, is he must now be here somewhere," I warned.

The tinkling of mounds of shells propelled back and forth in the tide against the shoreline rang out in my mind from tinkling, to ringing of sleigh bells, to loud ringing of warning bell, very loud.

A dozen dragonflies flew over the altar. A loud buzz roared right over our heads. I looked up to see if it was a swarm of dragonflies in the style of Alfred Hitchcock's "The Birds." A drone with a video camera hovered over us then glided toward land.

J pointed to the hammock on the deck above. A silhouette of a hunched over gaunt 60 ish man in jeans and a white t-shirt jumped up and ran towards Ocean Boulevard out of our sight.

"That's The Fugitive!" I screamed.

# CHAPTER 5
# POSSESSED

I don't know what possessed me, but I grabbed the blue design backpack, and started running towards the beach exit. It was in my possession, whatever it was. J ran with me. The adrenaline filled act felt surreal like we were in a reality TV show.

We darted down the beach oblivious to the sharp shells. My right foot left tiny pools of blood with each stride.

"What is going on?" he screamed.

A solo white frigate bird followed us. He appeared out of nowhere as frigates do. They normally fish offshore and signal sport fishermen where tuna, marlin and mahi feed below. The frigates dive for baitfish being pushed up by the larger predators below. This frigate fished in the shore break right beside us in a jerky random flight pattern, up and down, right and left, occasionally seeming to disappear altogether against the rising sun. His small bony aerodynamic frame was the size of a wood airplane toy from the 1960s.

I pointed and directed, "Stealth, fast, unpredictable moves."

"That's a bird! What are we doing?" he demanded.

"I don't know The Fugitive personally. He lived at the Port Lucaya Marina for several months in 2013. He was lurking around when we docked Blue Daze in November and was there still when I arrived for New Year's on another friend's boat. I stayed on Blue Daze and my friends docked next to me. The Fugitive spent his daytime hours roaming around the marina asking people if they were going to Costa Rica. He wanted a ride on a private vessel to Costa Rica. He started each day by leaving the creepy matching backpack on the picnic table by my boat and would pick it up at sunset. There are jewel-tone picnic tables on the docks where boaters gather and socialize," I said.

"I'm not hearing every word so you might have to repeat some of this," he muttered between heavy breaths.

I continued remembering New Year 2013 out loud between breaths, "Rumor on the dock, had it that he was living in the vacant Customs building on the second story overlooking the marina. Some people thought he was a spy or an escaped convict or just an insane ex-patriot. We nicknamed him The Fugitive. He had cash somehow. The dock master told someone he got a Federal Express package every Friday. Presumably, cash sent by someone. Who sent it was of great speculation by the boaters."

A tour bus from the Four Seasons in Manalapan on the southernmost tip of the island delivered a group of tourists. A clamoring of clicking of cameras greeted us at the public beach access. From under umbrellas, fully clothed Asians stood awkwardly in the thick sand.

"Maybe they snapped evidence of The Fugitive," I pointed.

We flew up the steps to the sidewalk, north on Ocean Boulevard two blocks to Worth Avenue and ran west towards the marina on the intercoastal just four blocks away.

"Let's board the boat at Brazilian Dock," I screamed as he was falling 10 feet behind me.

A bright green flock of screeching noisy parrots flew overhead right over the one and two story shops drowning out my directives. I stopped and repeated myself as he caught up.

"So, I hope those parrots had good news for us?" he nudged indulging my bird obsession of the day.

"The parrots live in the trees on Cocoanut Walk by The Breakers. The only time I notice them is in the late afternoon as they congregate back in the trees and socialize amongst each other. I ride my bike there late afternoons sometimes to be among them. So, I guess I would call that fly-by a message of the unusual," I speculated, much too distracted to really discern if it meant anything at all.

I crossed Worth and a neon lime green Lamborghini slammed on his brakes to avoid hitting me. You would think I would notice lime green and Lamborghini. A parade of more Lamborghinis, Ferraris and Porsches crawled on Worth with the upcoming Supercar Week festivities. We ran past the parallel parked Rolls, Bentleys, Austin Martins, of course Mercedes and BMWs, some with vanity tags and many in custom colors and trims. We crossed between Tiffany's and Chanel to Peruvian Avenue with less traffic, and puffed two more blocks. We ran past the mega-yacht dock to Brazilian Dock in the City Docks Marina. Flustered, I couldn't remember the code on the gate to the dock. Finally, it clicked open after four tries.

"Be careful, this metal dock is slippery when wet and look at the proximity to water! It's always wet!" I warned, after several spills myself.

The aluminum dock thundered under our stomping as we raced to the boat. We boarded the 60 foot Hateras and I pulled out my keys. The Girl Scout-always-prepared pink pirate backpack was as usual loaded for adventure, and the unexpected. I fumbled with the keys. The lock was old and tricky.

I made nervous small talk as I manipulated the lock, "We neighbor with only a few other sport fishing boats because most fishermen prefer Sailfish Marina. Sailfish is right by the Lake Worth Inlet. From here you have to go through two bridges, which can take hours for the bridges to be opened. Blue Daze is here because it's for sale and I used it for a floating condo before I rented my guesthouse. I love being right on the water. I love waking to the marina sounds. My son and his friends were here last month and we caught a boatload of mahi. It was so fun. It's not as safe here as you might think. West Palm Beach people row up small boats and do petty theft here at this marina. I keep it locked tight after the first round of coolers, hoses and lines disappeared," I rambled.

The engine room door was ajar, which I found odd, but continued inside to the galley. I gave a quick text to Captain Ed to check the engine room when he returned.

The boat interior had fresh carpet the color of the sand and new upholstery the color of sky. My client Owen had an extensive art collection that he rotated from his homes and the boat. He hung one of my fish paintings, which I felt honored among the fine art on the other walls. Everything inside sparkled as though it was new. The boat was Owen's pampered baby.

"It's coming back to me," I recalled more details of The Fugitive, "We did the three-hour crossing from Palm Beach to West End in the other sporty. Three weeks earlier, in Blue Daze we glided over with perfect glassy conditions. For New Year's it was raining but we killed the Wahoo. I caught two taller than I am. They put up a fight! The next day, which was New Year's Eve, we fished to Port Lucaya in the rain again."

I got water bottles from the galley refrigerator for us. We were both sweating profusely. J was nervous, really nervous. He shifted his weight from one leg to the other like a big flamingo.

"The others all started with the rum punch at lunch at Zorba's. Again, Ted is in Aspen every year, so I was by myself. We had agreed to meet at Rum Runners at 6 p.m. Count Basie Square pulsed with party-goers. Our meeting place was too crowded so they relocated across the square at another bar. I couldn't see them lost in the mob. They assumed I'd wander and find them. The cell tower was down, typical of Bahamas. Anyway, The Fugitive walks up to me after I sat there for 45 minutes by myself and asks me to have dinner with him. He had been staring at me and creeping me out. I tell him I'm waiting on my friends. He admitted he had been watching me, creepy right? He told me my friends left me. Thank God right about then the group showed up and found me for our dinner reservations at Sabor."

I continued, "In his offer to take me for dinner he showed me a giant wad of $100 bills saying 'See I have plenty of money.' I told him to take off his hat so I could see him. I wanted to identify who was about to kidnap me! I studied his face so I could describe it in detail to a criminal sketch artist. His hair was light brown and thinning on top and in a circle in back. His eyes were a hazel color embedded in a thin face. When I refused multiple times to have dinner with him, he told me we had to talk. He told me people in the U.S. wanted to kill him. He said he wanted to go to Guatemala, or Costa Rica, or anywhere in Central or South America. Then he told me he had a secret to tell me. So maybe that was true or maybe he's just insane. Looks like we are about to find out."

We opened the note in the sealed plastic bag. I read it aloud, "Not your imagination. Real. Destiny. The user name is the place you last saw me in all caps and no spaces. The password is the date of your first cyber stalking message, numeric with no symbols. I will communicate with you through the Notes app."

I looked up at J, "Oh my God! The Fugitive was a part of the 2011 and Unlucky-13 cyber stalker fiasco! I remember the date like my children's birthdays. Both changed my life forever, one for good, one for really, really bad."

From my backpack, I handed J a copy of my book "Marlins Cry A Phishing Story" and pointed to the introduction.

He started reading aloud, "June 12, 2011 ... The screen savers showed Word-of-the-day dictionary messages. I read them aloud to (Owen). 'Attenuate. Verb. Reduce the force, effect or value of. Reduce the amplitude of such as of a signal, electrical current, or other oscillation. Adj. Attenuated. Reduce the virulence of such as of a pathogenic organism or vaccine. Reduce in thickness. Make thin.' Another screen popped up and I read it aloud, 'Wrath. Noun. Extreme anger chiefly used for humorous or rhetorical effect.' Another screen saver popped up as I finished reading that one and again, I read it aloud, 'Westering. Adj. especially of the sun nearing the west.'"

Stunned, he exclaimed, "Damn Cat Sunshine, it sounds like this cyber guy wants to put you out of orbit!"

I rolled my eyes and sarcastically responded, "Really? You think?"

He asked, "I thought you were a ghost writer?"

"I am now. Before 2011, I was a serious magazine publisher, promoter, filmmaker and emerging author. I try to keep a low profile now. Read that book and you will understand. Looks like you are in the sequel now, my friend. Should we open this backpack?" I asked, already unzipping the top.

"You are too brazen. Maybe we shouldn't get involved. We should take this package to the police," he cowered.

"The police can't help in cyber crimes until we have proof. The laws and processes all protect the cyber criminals. It's too early. Officials want 'hard evidence' so we need to get that before we get them involved. Trust me," I snipped annoyed.

I pulled out an iPhone, the only contents.

I put the iPhone on the counter in the galley. I lifted the top, and made sure Wi-Fi, Bluetooth, and other connectors were disabled. We both stared at the screen as I put in the user name "PORTLUCAYA." I put in the password, "061211."

The screen saver was the same ocean wave photo I had used on my MacBook Pro in 2011. There was only one note in the Notes app. I took a deep breath and clicked on it to open it.

I read the document out loud like J couldn't just read it himself. I almost couldn't read it because his nose was an inch from the monitor. It read, "I'm a friend of the family. I have information for you for your writing."

I looked at my two-tone stainless and gold Omega watch, and it was 11:11 a.m.

"The word 'family' has significance for me J. It was a key spiritual concept given to me," I explained.

"What does that mean? I don't understand," said J.

"Maybe this guy is a wacko and he's hacked into my computer to read my journals. Here, read this," I said.

I opened my Notes app on my iPhone and opened a page titled "I Want A Family."

J read aloud, "June 30, 1996, God said clearly, 'I Want A Family.' The voice came from the pew behind me. It was a man's voice. No man or any person was near us. Sermon notes: God is more likely to intervene supernaturally when ... 1) A great promise has been made, 2) a great faith is present, 3) a great cause is attempted, 4) a great point needs to be made."

He took a deep breath and turned his head to the side and stared at my face.

"Cat, 1996? You certainly are patient. I hope you are a Saint and not a sucker," he said shaking his head.

"My twin soul, my forever love, is worth the wait," I said without hesitation.

## CHAPTER 6
## PICKET FENCE PONDERINGS

I had a full January planned with birthday travels and celebrations. Since client Owen wasn't filling my time with work projects, I found lots of play projects. My friends and supporters grew weary of the topic of cyber security in 2011 and again in 2013. I decided I would not bring this topic up with anyone this time.

I threw the creepy backpack in the trash. We hid The Fujitive's iPhone in the storage space under the stairs leading to the master stateroom. We locked the boat and walked to our places on the ocean side of the island just a few blocks away.

"I'm meeting Ann to pick her up from the Chesterfield. I've got to run. Don't tell anyone about our secret. Let's call it The Project. That's generic enough," I instructed.

J's guesthouse was a block away from mine. As he said goodbye, he added, "I'm supposed to leave for New York for a soap opera gig I got for January. I'm staying here to support you."

I responded, "No. Do your work. Keep life as normal as possible. Life can get un-normal in an instant. I lived through 2011 and 2013 cyber attacks to attest to this known fact," I said.

The curly tail sentry greeted me at my guesthouse. He didn't move as he usually did, so I tried not to crush him. As a result, I tripped up the stairs and bloodied my shin. I was a wounded mess.

I sat on the corner of my bed, and opened my purse and pulled out a Post-It note from 2013 that read, "Dwell upon that which is L. Lovely, E. Enlightened, N. Noble, S. Serene. LENS." The energy triggered my mind to remember to see the world through God's LENS. It was my soul's purpose, like a lens, to spread and disperse light.

The LENS single word messages were from Y during the 2013 scary era. I was given one word at a time that was specific to events of the cyber abuse drama. The affirmation also calmed me in times of unrest of any kind after the attack.

I took a deep breath and asked Y to protect me in white light. I pictured the army of angels over my dwelling. Also, during cyber stalking, Y told me in Marsh Harbour Bahamas at Boat Harbour that I should not be concerned for my safety because, "You have the protection of the wings of one thousand angels. Look up. Protecting them are one thousand more for every star of the sky." You don't have to write down that affirmation. The power of that visual stays with you.

I showered and got myself together.

Ted called, "Hola Senora Gato! Hi Cat! Practicing my Spanish. Can't wait for our Costa Rica trip. I'm missing you big. Calling you from Ajax. If you are online, look at me on Aspen Mountain live webcam. I'm blowing you a big kiss! Fresh powder! Everything good there? Antsy there yet?"

"All is wonderful in paradise," I somewhat fabricated, after all, I was in paradise and things were 90 percent wonderful.

We made small talk for a few minutes. I pulled a Pee Wee Herman move from "Pee Wee's Big Adventure" when he made crackle sounds so he could hang up on Dottie and I said, "The wind must be really blowing because I'm having a hard time hearing you."

Words have power so why not convince myself all is well? Why worry him and besides, there was nothing to be concerned about, just some note from a nutcase. Ted called my best friend Ann "Antsy" because she flitted from man to man. She could because she was strikingly stunning. She worked at it with constant beauty regiments and procedures. We had a similar look with long straight blonde hair and blue eyes. She was glam. On the other hand, I could swim in the ocean without concern for the massacre of hair extensions, fake eye lashes or spray tan. Her breast augmentation beat mine by two sizes and she dressed to impress, starting with cleavage. We didn't compete for men ever in our 40 year friendship because we would attract different types of men.

One of her beaus was arriving the next week, so instead of staying with me at the guest house on my sleeper sofa, he set her up at the luxury boutique Chesterfield Hotel on the island. She didn't like her hair extensions blown around, so I drove to meet her leaving the convertible top up on my new 3 Series BMW. The salt from the ocean breeze was caked in a thick layer, like icing on a cupcake with big crusty patches. I smeared it with the windshield wipers as best I could and drove a few blocks with blurred visibility. On the one-way streets, I had to go to Ocean Boulevard to turn to the next street to go west. A group of 100 bicyclists whizzed by with their helmets tucked low and their tight black Lycra shorts hugging their tone bodies. The cyclists usually biked the island on Sunday mornings when there was virtually no traffic. On Sunday mornings, the religious people are at church, the heathens are sleeping off their hangovers, and the workers have the day off. The roads are empty. Another anomaly, another cluster of two-wheeled vehicles whizzed by but with a deafening roar of mufflers. A Harley pack suited in black leather, facial hair and tattoos passed by. Clearly the costumed revelers were headed south to Delray or another more suitable party town for them. Palm Beach only has Charley's Crab and The Breakers Hotel on the ocean, and both are more white linen than black leather. Other than an occasional Vespa, it was the first time I saw motorcycles on The Island.

There was no parking on Cocoanut Row. I circled back to South County and wiggled into a two hour space. Most of the time my car sat in my space at the guesthouse or my garage in Winter Park. The only miles I put on it were the 500 Turnpike miles bouncing back and forth between my two residences.

Ann called, "Hey, I'm running late. You know, you love this island. Why don't you sell your house and move to Palm Beach County?"

"I think about it all the time. I've looked at several options. I can't move until I know for sure," I said.

"Remember when I bought the Winter Park house? I had sold the marital home. I had renovated a five-bedroom three-bath home and had a contract on that one with a generous profit. Y showed me a vision of a picket fence. The homes I looked at didn't have that fence. The realtor called me a few short weeks before the kids and I had to move. She said she was parked in front of a house that just came on MLS listings. She said it was really cute and asked if I would I like to see it. I asked if it had a picket fence. She said, yes, it had one on the side yard. I told her, 'OK then. Prepare a contract for the asking price and I will meet you there tomorrow.' She said, 'But I haven't told you the address or the price.' I responded, 'You wouldn't be telling me about it if it wasn't in my price range and in the kids' school district. It has the picket fence, so I will live there.' I moved in the week after 9/11," I continued.

"I forgot that story. You always follow your visions. So, get your 'know' mojo on for a house here," pushed Ann.

"We can plot the latitude and longitude of the next picket fence when you get here," I suggested.

The human psyche craves solo time. As much as I was excited to have Ann around, I relished a few minutes of me time. Mojo shows up when it's me not we.

# CHAPTER 7
# MONKEY AND A DOG

I settled into a back corner table at the Leopard Lounge. Antsy was always late. She had a ridiculous list of things to do to get ready to leave the house. I planned to catch up on e-mails with my iPhone. I rarely used Wi-Fi, so I could tune into my online life anywhere using cell minutes on my excessively large data plan. I learned that your phone is more vulnerable to hacking on shared public Wi-Fi.

The Leopard Lounge was right out of the 1920s with rich dark reds and black varnish, and, of course, leopard print. I occupied myself for a few minutes with the art of naked ladies on the ceiling. I found an image that made me think of Ted and another that made me think of Tennis Player.

The other venue that had naked lady art on the ceiling would be the antithesis of Leopard Lounge, Wally's on Mills Avenue in Orlando. Wally's poured strong drinks for 50 cents back in my college days. The smoke-filled dive bar kept a full parking lot around the clock of underage drinkers, and all age groups who remember the first drink they had at Wally's, and the hard core ashen colored alcoholics who swear that, "Wally's is a good deal."

A painting on the wall of a monkey and a dog captured my attention. Monkeys are a big theme in Palm Beach. The famous 1920s architect developer Addison Mizner dressed his spider monkey Johnnie in elaborate costumes like the one in the painting. There were few patrons and my section was empty. I moved to a table closer to the art to study the rich oil composition. The costumed animals both faced me, not each other. The monkey had the dog on a loose leash.

"Who is in charge?" Y asked me.

I pulled out a pen and the small journalist notebook I kept in my Chanel shopper bag. I could feel insights from Y flowing from the questions I had asked earlier on the beach walk that were postponed by J.

I watched as my pen stroked the crisp white paper, "The dog could seek the thrill of a chase with a squirrel. The dog could fancy a small animal and easily overpower the monkey. The monkey could yearn to soar with a bird high in the sky, and meet him in a towering palm. The monkey could simply put the leash down and seek to fly. Life by design is in perfect balance. So, as one action is taken, so yet another action follows. Life is a choice to be in balance. Choices are only half yours between a monkey and a dog. Neither the dog nor the monkey is in charge of each other, but definitely, each is in charge of themselves."

"Cat!" squealed Ann as she threw her arms around my neck.

I was unaware of her in the room. When I get in 'the zone' I am unaware of much else.

"The hotel put me in a suite. I've got a bedroom, a sitting room with a pullout sofa, and two full baths. All the rooms are tiny here but since I'm staying a week, they upgraded me. Hey, I'm craving that crispy grouper sandwich at the Colony. Let's go there and do lunch at the Bimini Bar by the pool," she suggested.

I convinced her it was just a few blocks so we walked to visit my favorite poolside café. The pool lounge chairs were filled with sunning ladies in jewel tone one-piece swim suits that matched the Bimini Bar where Ann and I found bar stools. All the ladies were reading the Shiny Sheet behind large black sunglasses under large wide-brimmed straw hats. They had fruity cocktails in plastic cups held by hands with wedding rings no less than ten-carats each. The rings sparkled in the midday sun.

"Looks like they all went shopping together, huh?" Ann commented with a smirk.

She was always aware of other women around her. She was the fashion police. She monitored fashion and bling.

"Their husbands must be golfing or fishing or other men things. So, we are no less single than they are when you really get down to it," she declared as the mid-twenties Ken-doll bartender addressed us with a wide bleached smile.

"Two champagnes, best in the house, and a crispy grouper sandwich to split," she ordered for me, turning back to me, "I don't want to get fat by myself. No salad for you Missy."

"Tennis anyone?" she inquired smugly.

A text dinged from my iPhone.

"That's him now," I said, "He wants to meet us for drinks at The Steak Out before dinner. OK with you?"

"Sure, I'd love to give him a little flirt before I have to kick in New Year's Resolutions," she said and continued, "I'm going to only date my new guy for all of this year. He's the best boyfriend ever."

She always vowed exclusivity in new relationships. The newbie always held the title 'the one.' She was attractive and flirtatious. The men would try so hard at first to please her before they blew it with her. So, it was no wonder she always had such high hopes for each one. Unlike me, if things went south, she healed and moved on quickly.

"I'm going to fulfill my life's purpose and find my twin soul for this lifetime," I said.

"You always say that resolution. Still looking for Harrison Gore?" she asked amused.

"We're looking for each other. I have quite a resume on HG now after trying to find him all this time," I said.

"Remember when I was divorcing right after you? Remember we went to that Spiritualist Camp Cassadaga on the way to New Smyrna Beach? Well, everything that woman told me in that historic hotel came true. And your man was going to be a cross between Harrison Ford and Al Gore, thus Harrison Gore," she laughed.

"I wasn't supposed to meet him till after my fiftieth year, and I was supposed to have up to a dozen relationships before finding him, something that freaked me out as a woman in my mid-thirties who had slept with only one man!" I reminisced.

"Maybe you got my reading about the dirty dozen!" she laughed.

"You know, I started after the divorce with a qualifier that I didn't want stepchildren with baby teeth. Now I'm looking for no dependent children. I may have to wait until the no dentures era!" I laughed.

"Ted is my soul mate, for this era. When I had the cyber attacks, he wasn't by my side, but he had my back. He threw money at the problem. He hired and paid for the ex-CIA guys who did the forensic work. I appreciate him. I would have liked for him to be with me instead of in the Bahamas and France. It was my problem, not his," I said.

"So, what about the stalker? How about we place an online dating ad with his profile and describe him as 'very attentive' and 'likes to surprise you' and..." she laughed.

"You are so funny! Stalker is out of the picture, and more importantly, I'm out of his picture!" I brushed off the topic even though baggage from that era was currently stashed on the boat. The Fugitive might not have anything to do with the past cyber stalker. It possibly was all fresh drama. It hopefully was nothing at all.

"Another skinny margarita! You remember the way I like it ..." a 70-something yapped at the bartender in a thick raspy Boston accent while pushing Ann's back with her voluminous Ralph Lauren beach bag.

I asked, "Did you hear about the produce aisle wars at Publix? You get the big dogs from this place and that place all expecting to be treated like royalty as they are 'back home.' They get here and are surrounded by other big dogs. They point their fingers and growl at each other and then the finger biting starts," I dramatized for her, as we laughed and the margarita was served.

Ann ordered a second champagne while I paced myself.

"Let's hit Chanel because I scratched my sunglasses ... again!" I suggested.

"I could use some retail therapy myself," she agreed.

"Ted claimed he didn't know what to give me for Christmas, so he gave me a card and a stack of Ben Franklins to shop for myself. He stopped choosing gifts for me," I mused.

"Because he already bought you so much so early on in your relationship! You need to grow more fingers for all the diamonds and sapphires. Look at your bling! Shopping is fun anyway," she quipped.

Worth was frenzied with last minute holiday shopping. I convinced Ann again that we could walk since Worth was only a block away and her hair wouldn't get frizzy.

On the sidewalk, an elderly man pushed a doggie stroller with a bejeweled Maltese with one hand and held a diamond-filled hand of what must have been his first wife. They were on the flat-shoe-shuffle stage of life now. It was possible to find and keep true love. The lucky ones find each other earlier in life. The lovebirds weren't bored at all with one another. Quite the contrary, the two beamed like lovestruck newlyweds. He wore a pink tie to match her Lilly dress. I used to dress my baby daughter in the same manner with matching Lilly outfits. I could dictate a baby's wardrobe much like this woman looked like she could dictate wardrobe or just about anything to her adoring mate. When Ted and I first dated, at the San Francisco Ritz at breakfast every morning on the concierge level, the other jealous couples called us "The Love Birds." I'm certain at least two of the couples that week increased their romance starting with, "Why don't we do that anymore?" The women smiled more at me the second and third mornings over coffee. They still teased us about the lovebird thing.

"Cat! Cat! Cat! Say hello to Armando," Ann poked me and woke me from my daydreaming.

She was exchanging numbers with Worth's version of the Ambercrombie model-greeter. The Paris and LA shirtless versions translate on Worth to Armani blue suits with crisp white linen shirts. They work for the jewelry store across from Ta-boo, and flirt as well as provide security.

"Armando's an Uber driver in the evenings. He can drive us around tonight. He's available because he just broke up with his girlfriend. Can you imagine her letting this one get away? And he's got a boat and wants to take us fishing this week," she flirted and batted her eyes at what looked like a 20-something my son's age. At least we had our transportation set, although taxis at night are always plentiful on the island.

We continued walking and I reminded Ann, "I don't really like fishing. I like yachting. Translated, that means a captain or mate to bait, gaff, unhook, ice and clean the fish. I like to reel in fish and take photos and videos. I like to write about them, too!"

Ann offered, "You just never know around here. He might have a cooler boat than Owen's. I'm sure it's not a leaking rowboat! I'll scope out the details before I commit us."

"Remember when we were in Sardinia for the sailing yacht races at Porto Cervo? I was looking for Armando then. I named my soul mate Armando and we asked all the Mediterranean gorgeous men that week if they knew him. Then we would take our photos with potential Armando contenders. The question was a great ice-breaker. The European men 'got' that looking for a soul mate is a noble cause. Remember?" I asked.

"Yes, then the bartender at the end of the week in his adorable Italian accent told you, 'Charlotte, you haven't found Armando in Italy because it's a Spanish name so Armando certainly is in Spain! Next trip you need to choose an Italian name for your fictitious soul mate.' What's our opening line tonight?" she asked.

"Pretty simple, ask about resolutions, that will tell you a lot about someone," I responded.

A Worth Avenue window-shopping walk was like speed dating the best of the world's most exclusive and exquisite designer brands, boutiques and art galleries. In a gallery window, a Calder sculpture of circus trapeze performers reminded me of my relationship with Ted with me hanging in the balance. Everything reminded me of Ted.

The pampered Maltese now was sipping from one of the many decorated adorned doggie bowls built into the tiles of the historic Mediterranean shops. They were by Tiffany's.

I replaced my scratched polarized sunglasses at Chanel. I destroyed or lost glasses on the boat four times this year. Across the street at Island Company, I got fresh flip-flops and a sarong for my upcoming trip with Ted to Costa Rica. I'm efficient at shopping. I use my intuition to walk directly to the rack or shelf or display of the item I am to buy. I put the rest of the cash back in my Christmas card from Ted and met Ann shopping in Ralph Lauren.

"If I stray I can't stay," I said.

"That's random. What's that mean?" she asked.

"You know, I married the first guy I slept with. Shockingly, I was right out of college and he was right out of law school. I always had this vision of how my life would be as a couple and I committed to that early on in my life. I'm basically conservative. But in ten years, I've not been fully loyal to Ted, not that I should. I'm feeling guilty about Tennis Player. I've been on dates with him, but last night was the first time we were intimate. He was my camouflage pretend date the last few months so you guys would all stop bugging me about dating. In my past, if I cheated, it would signal myself to end a relationship. For me, it would be the end of a commitment," I confessed.

"Did you enjoy playing tennis?" she asked.

"Our chemistry is crazy," I answered.

"Then stop feeling anything but giddy with your hunky distraction. Be giddy not guilty! Ted is not your soul mate," she advised.

"My spiritual advisor Molly told me out of my 200 or so past lives, yes 200, that Ted was in several of them. In one, he was a doting father and farmer in the Midwest who worked hard to send me, his only child to college. He died while I was gone, so I need to repay him and see him through old age in this life. In another life, I was a nurse and he was injured in combat and I took care of him till he died, so he's back to complete the love affair that got cut short. Soul mate doesn't imply only, I have many soul mates. The karma with Ted has been worked out in our time together. I do feel we have fulfilled our purposes with each other. I hope we can transition to friends. He is my best friend, other than you, of course," I said.

"This is the first I've heard of you considering letting him go. Are you OK?" she asked.

"We have to put on our party faces, let's talk tomorrow about Ted," I said and we walked in separate directions to get on our sequins, stilettos and hair spray.

King Midas called to wish me a Happy New Year. He was in The

Keys with a date. His voice made me smile. I stopped in front of the Vineyard Vines store to talk to him. The window radiated with island apparel. In my mind, I was wearing the sundress in the window and with him on an ocean-view patio. I had to admit he still made my heart flutter when I saw his name pop up on my caller ID. I blew it with him years ago because I wouldn't let Ted go. King Midas was not the type to share a girlfriend. Someone else was his date in the sundress now. She was likely very young. "Life is full of choices. I'm actually lucky I've had so many choices," I thought.

As I passed Ta-boo, the love birds were dining in the coveted open window table by the sidewalk. There was a Tiffany teal blue box with white satin bow by her iced tea. They were still holding hands.

# CHAPTER 8
# HEALINGS

The cuts on my right foot from the shells compounded with the bruise on the shin from the stair trip, made dressing in my black short dress problematic. I pulled out a tea-length dress that I wore to a Mar-a-Lago charity gala last fall. I didn't worry if I wore formal dresses more than once. I was with all different people. And, I assumed that nobody paid that close of attention to me anyway. I hid the bruise sufficiently but the Band-aid stuck out of my strappy black Manolo Blahniks. Ann gave them to me for Christmas. She was a big online shopper and insisted these were my New Year's must-wear heels.

I sat on my teal leather sleeper-sofa. It faced a sliver of ocean of the same color outside of my living room window. I asked Y for healing. I meditated for a minute tuning into my healing powers that I assume everyone must have. I put my palms an inch apart until I felt the warmth of the energy flowing between the two palms. I placed my right palm on my bruised shin and concentrated on healing for a few minutes.

I was with Ted during one healing. He was a huge part of my history with numerous uncanny events and spiritual revelations. Trying to explain my life to a new lover would be dicey as he might think I was crazy. Ted wasn't particularly spiritual but he accepted that I was and marveled at the events he witnessed first-hand by my side. On one Bahamas fishing trip, off Harbour Island on Eleuthera, I grasped a red snapper to hold for a photo. I was wearing big yellow protective gloves but the fish squirmed and poked my left forearm with his fins. By the next morning my forearm was black and blue and bloating. We went to the airport as planned to arrive in Fort Lauderdale late afternoon. I insisted we drive from there back to Winter Park in case I needed emergency care, I wanted to be closer to home.

On the four hour drive, Y told me to take a photo of the wound. I assumed it was to document for emergency workers. I listened as Y told me to zoom in on the photo. I did and there was a distinct line of red punctures left by the red snapper fin. I showed the enlarged photo to Ted. He suggested, "Probably the fish was in contact with a lion fish which is highly poisonous. Or even bacteria on the coral reefs can be hazardous to humans." So, we determined what was likely wrong. My willowy slender arm had grown to the size of a football.

I meditated and asked Y to heal me. In giving massages to Ted, he insisted that I could heal his aching muscles and claimed my massages were better than any he had anywhere in the world. We had a lot of couples massages in spas all over the place. I could run my palms an inch from his back and he could tell me where my hands were by the healing sensation. So, I used the long drive to place my palm on my arm. By the time, we arrived in Winter Park, Ted dropped me off at my house rather than the emergency room. The arm was still bright red, but had shrunk back to normal size. Ted was in awe. I was relieved. I took photos the next day of a bright white imprint of my right hand on the red bruised arm.

Now, several years later, I looked down and rolled my arms to the left and right in front of me. The scars were totally invisible on my left arm.

On my right wrist, my earliest memory of a wound still left a white wide scar. I was pre-school age. An older neighbor boy offered a ride on his banana-seat bike, an irresistible offer to a biker still dependent upon training wheels. I dutifully held his glass jar he was taking to the lake to catch tadpoles. He pedaled up a driveway. He wiped out and we fell down onto the concrete shattering the glass as it sliced through my wrist. I have a memory of the emergency room and the horrid sight of the fleshy bloody meat inside my white skin. It was a close call for my life as I could have bled to death in my little white sailor-trimmed two-piece swim suit.

On that same hand, when I was in high school, my surfboard fin sliced through my lifeline on my palm causing more stitches. Palm readers through the years wince at the scar and tell me I'm lucky to be alive. I was happy the surfboard severed my hand and not my face where the torpedo shaped fiberglass board was headed. Besides being on the top three any given year of lightning strike capital of the world, Florida also ranks in top tier for shark bites. I look back at my athletic youthful self, and consider my life to be spared and blessed.

I reclined on my bed with my feet dangling and closed my eyes. A strong visual image came to me from a fashion photo shoot for my magazine in 2010. We were shooting at a restaurant between lunch and dinner crowds so we had limited time. I was scurrying around the set holding jewelry for the models. I slipped on a slick wood floor, crumbled to my knees and slid 15 feet. When the shock wore off, I thought I had broken both of my ankles. I wasn't sure I could walk. The pearls from the necklace shot like bullets in all directions of the restaurant.

Y told me, "You are throwing your pearls before swine."

The message was right out of the Bible. I could feel Y's intense presence. It was the same type of message that Donna had told me years earlier but this time it came directly from the energy source. I felt physically the immediate stop of action in the room. Everything went to slow motion. In extreme pain, unable to walk, from there I crawled onto a bar stool and I completed the direction of the photo shoot without moving. Interestingly, both of the models, whom I considered friends, were concerned about their hair and makeup but showed zero interest in my swollen foot or the fact that I could not walk.

What appeared almost immediately were two distinct images in the wound. Very clearly a one inch cross appeared in my flesh. Above the cross was another symbol.

After the photo shoot, I healed my ankle within a week. The magazine would take longer. I had hoped to sell the brand so I kept it alive in a scaled down version. I began weaning my resources of time and effort from the magazine. It was a long process.

Five years later, recently in 2015, as I was cleaning my office files, I ran across the wound photo from 2010. I showed it to Margaret during a session I booked to help me with guidance for career, home and love in the New Year. I plucked the scribbled notes from my journal binder. I played her words back like a video in my head.

She glanced at the photo and said, "Extravagant cross! The infinity symbol is at an angle. It means 'love is forever.' Divine message. You cannot break a relationship based in infinity. It looks like a sideways number eight, or two intersecting circles. On you, the infinity symbol is just above the cross like a crown of thorns. The bond is forever. Your strength comes from the Divine. Never question your quest in this life. Your crowning energy will guide you. The cross represents hardship, crucifixion type events: your immense struggles both earthly and spiritually. You are Divinely aligned. You cannot fail."

I told her about Y's message that accompanied the wound and the symbols, "You are throwing pearls before swine."

"You have indeed been delaying your blessings," Margaret advised as I counted the delayed years on my fingers 'five.' That was just for the career part of my life. I would need more than my two hands to count the years of delay in my love life.

# CHAPTER 9
# LOVE IS FOREVER

Margaret started enlightening me on spiritual topics nearly 20 years ago. We have a friendship that pops up purposely in my spiritual growth periods. I was separating from my husband with two young children in tow. I had many questions. I had questions about my life, and even more questions about what was happening to me spiritually. As I prayed and asked for guidance, I heard God's voice very clearly. I called upon my New Age friend for knowledge of such things. Direct messages from the spirit world filled the Bible, so it didn't conflict with my Christian religious beliefs necessarily. People around me, however, were oppressive and opposed my curiosity. Nonetheless, I chose along the way, to obey each message given directly to me, even when the advice seemed counter intuitive.

Margaret assured me that I was not crazy, that God was simply answering my prayers. She assured me that there was indeed good and evil in the spirit world, but my experiences were good. She said I had a gift that I did hear Spirit so clearly, not a curse. She said some people go through life and have no spiritual experiences. Some people may have one. The fact that my messages were flooding in daily in profound and significant ways, were to be taken seriously. Spirit wanted me to know something.

Margaret took me for several dinners around that period to TuTu Tango, a tacky restaurant on touristy International Drive in Orlando. The restaurant had artists painting, belly dancing, and psychics and tarot card readers. We would take notes for each other while getting readings, then discuss the readings over dessert after dinner.

I recently had copied notes from my journals of what I considered significant moments and consolidated them into one notebook. I was trying to downsize and organize my life, including my piles and piles of notes. One event that made significant-status happened in the middle of this zany restaurant. It was the second reading I had at TuTu with Margaret.

I got the notebook of favorites, and looked up the reading from June 13, 1996 that I named "Love is Forever." The notes read:

"Previous life. Healthy and positive. Green Mother. Many children. Healer with herbs and trees around one main tree. Psychic and telepathic. In Europe. Children would help gather mushrooms. Wild pigs around. All sizes of blonde children running around in forest cheerful and serious about helping you. Where's your man? Goes to village. Big, huge with long blonde hair. Something cut off the activity. Happy ideal life cut short. The church didn't understand and didn't like the healing. The husband comes back and there's nothing left. He's enraged and bellowing. The tree where people brought gifts and treasures, he drops in front of to his knees. You come out of the tree as a beautiful white spirit and caress his head in your hands and you tell him, 'You can't destroy love. Love is forever.' Rainbow card. Choose happily ever after. We make our destiny. Like the bad fairy sentences Cinderella to death when she pricks her finger and the good fairy says she will only sleep. This is all a test of your courage. There is nothing left to learn other than love is everything. You already learned that and you chose to come back in this life out of love. Your sole purpose is love. Push for love and passion. It doesn't die."

"Love is forever. And, love is taking forever to find me indeed!" I thought, and I counted 20 years since Margaret took those notes for me.

This reading resonated with me. I had visions of this prior life in this life. It came to me in my dreams. It came to me in my desires. When I visited Europe in my freshman year of college, places I had never been in this life seemed quite familiar, very familiar.

## CHAPTER 10
## SIXTH SENSE IN SIXTH GRADE

I wrote about my past-life memories in my childhood, until society made me self-conscious by an experience in sixth grade.

I can remember at a very young age sitting in the back of a Baptist Church or Presbyterian Church and when the minister would talk about being born again, I literally thought he meant born again, as in reincarnation. I remembered quite a bit from past lives.

My dad called me Tinkerbell. He said I was like a little fairy. I was quiet and always creating art projects or writing, so my mother said I was an easy child to raise.

"The opening was getting bigger and bigger." That was the opening line to an essay for testing in sixth grade. We responded to three or four opening lines that year as a homework project. My essay was about the sun peeking through the clouds. I described in great detail morning glories. I described in delicate intricacy flora and fauna not found in Florida. I can still smell the fragrance of the petals and touch the dew on the leaves as I recall this scene. It wasn't a scene from Florida. I channeled a scene from a significant event from a past life influencing this life. The garden was a joyful scene before tragedy would cut that life short. My soul recalled the details.

This was hard to explain as a child. It is hard to explain now. It was excruciatingly hard to explain to the school principal. My straight-A honor society self was called to the principal's office where my parents were waiting.

"Did you write her essay for her? Did some other adult help her? There is no way a sixth grader could have written this," the inquisition began.

My parents assured that I did write the essay, and that I wrote all the time. I had a special talent they explained to the admonishing administrator.

In fourth and fifth grade the same school educated me in a special class for high-testing bright students where we independently taught ourselves at our own pace. As a Type-A, I diligently completed academic tasks and had abundant time to use the plethora of art supplies. I had ample time to write short stories and create pretend magazines. The creativity the school nurtured in me for two years, in sixth grade, they now wanted to squash.

I was shy and reserved anyway. I was embarrassed. I still got A's but was OK with B's now. I wouldn't put as much effort into homework from that point forward. Most kids don't want to feel different. I didn't want to stand out especially after being embarrassed. I didn't want to have to explain what I barely understood myself. I felt like a misfit in a land of Martians of another species. My mother understood me. I loved her very much. I would continue to write but only share it at home.

As for my sixth sense, at that time, I wished it to be eighty-sixed, restaurant lingo for finished.

# CHAPTER 11
# JUST IN CAYCE 1996

I flipped the page of my journal notebook to my first TuTu reading the previous month on May 2, 1996. This reading spurred a quest of knowledge and thought before the internet. I bought paperback books of Edgar Cayce the modern-day seer, to further my understanding. I read them cover-to-cover by the pool as my children swam in our backyard pool. When I moved from the marital home, I didn't move the books with me. I'm not sure if this vision by this card reader was read correctly, but, nonetheless, it gave me a direction for further spiritual study. Until we are again in the afterlife, we will never really know the truth of a past life, or this life for that matter.

The notes Margaret took for me on May 2, 1996, saved in my notebook, read:

"Wheel of Fortune is power card. You had a previous life. (She laughed and added, 'This is so strange.') Doctor, couldn't read, you had four angels working with you. They did research and told you what to say. You were a sleeping prophet. (Margaret interrupted and said, 'Edgar Cayce, the sleeping profit.') Yeah, that's it. You had a childhood illness that is still with you. It's a pattern when something bothers you, you sleep and figure out your problems. There is something you don't want to talk about. You are a very private person and you are not sure who you can tell. When you share your secret, all of the cards will not be upside down. (She went into the marriage conflict.) Take heart, you are on a spiritual journey. Everything is going to be fine. The person you want really exists. He's a wonderful father. He's a wonderful husband. Supportive. Understanding. When you do the work, then you get security and power and you won't care what people think or say. Do you want to say when you are 80, I lived my life and I learned a lot or I played it safe and was boring?"

I asked her, "Why did you laugh at the beginning of the vision?"
She responded, "I usually get a vision of a previous life. I go in and can look through that person's eyes and describe the area. In this case, a voice was so excited like 'hurry up and tell her this,' and she told me what to tell you. The spirit is a she, and always with you. Ancient."

I went home from my girls-night-out dinner and read the notes to my then husband reading law books. He said he knew he was not that man. That was the end. The divorce would take several years of separation. Our spiritual bond was confirmed on my end of the relationship to be ended then.

Now all of this self-exploration seems rather indulgent for a mother of two young children looking at single life and a business with no client billings. It actually was necessary. I have always been able to manifest wishes. I truly had everything I had ever wanted, or ever thought to request of the Universe so far. I was a stay at home mom in an affluent idyllic setting, with adorable babies. I had a business for a creative outlet when I felt like working. It looked dreamy from outside of my Park Grove neighborhood oak tree lined brick road.

The reality is I woke one day in my seemingly perfect situation and my first thought was, "I'm still breathing." I wasn't too happy about it. Life had become unbearable to pretend I was happy or that family life as I was projecting to the public was my forever. I felt like a total failure although I had over achieved every goal I had ever set for myself ... except a happy lasting marriage. Through grace, I've never experienced that low sensation again.

At an annual checkup with my doctor, whom was also a friend asked me how I was, a normal question for a checkup. I burst into tears. He was friends with my husband. He told me, "You don't have to feel this way. I can prescribe antidepressants for you." I turned down the offer. I didn't want to be depressed and anxious but I didn't want to be numb either. The women I knew who resorted to mood enhancers to stay married seemed worse off than my sad situation. I choose knowing over numbing. I didn't understand how I could fix what I couldn't feel.

It was a quirky time when everything fell apart at once. I had two children, quit my successful career to stay at home, moved, renovated the new house, beat melanoma, lost both parents, family fell apart, and marriage tanking.

I also had some girls from the mean-girl-school turn on me as they do. Some of their husbands predictably hit on me, something I didn't want, and especially not from them. Women unintentionally push their husbands away by being mean to other women. Men innately are protectors.

Dates with single men were not an issue. I was 35 and looked 25. I started with a few light dinner dates with Rollins College graduate students. They thought they met a cougar but I was more like a kitten. It was painfully awkward as I had no dating experience past 22-years-old. Before getting engaged at that young age, I didn't sleep with anyone. After being allowed to date at 16, I had lots of dates through college until I got engaged, but nobody wanted to be a boyfriend for long to a girl in the late 1970s and early 1980s who wasn't going to be sexual.

That moment of "still breathing" was pivotal for me to seek my purpose and my path. My quest was necessary for survival. I immediately felt a strength and determination that was not my own. Y became my confidant. He provided big bold answers as only a supreme being could. When I prayed, my prayers were answered in profound ways. To ward off any spirits with ill intentions, I asked that God make sure that I knew the messages and inner urgings were coming from Him, and to make sure that I could not possibly misunderstand Him.

Around that time, my deceased father sat on the edge of my bed in spirit form and told me he would take care of my mother who was ill and would soon pass. I had prophetic dreams. I asked my husband how his grandmother was doing to his shock because he hadn't told me she was in the hospital. There were many, many, many incidents of my spirituality racing to warp speed. Like riding in a Nascar race car or a rocket, the speed made me a little nervous but I was seatbelted in and ready for the ride. Let's go!

# CHAPTER 12
## I WANT A FAMILY

I flipped to the next page of my journal notebook of "The Highlights of Cat's Life."
I had put an edited version of this experience in my Notes app in my iPhone. It was central to my spiritual purpose in this life. The entry dated June 30, 1996 was titled, "I want a family." It was written while I was sitting in church with my husband at the time and my preschool son who didn't like Sunday School. They offered five colored crayons. He was bored. I had a whole art room for him at home. If you want kids to sit in Sunday School and listen to stories of a far-off place 2,000 years ago, you should make it interesting. I believe the churches try harder now.

I WANT A FAMILY, June 30, 1996, the notes read:

"When I hurriedly sat on the pew, my usual five minutes late, before I oriented myself to the other worshippers or gathered my hymnal and Bible, God wasted no time. God said clearly, 'I want a family.' The voice came from the pew behind me. It was a man's voice. No man or any live person was near us."

I noted the sermon notes, which were racy for a conservative Presbyterian church at that time.

I noted, "The sermon was God is more likely to intervene supernaturally when ... 1) A great promise has been made, 2) a great faith is present, 3) a great cause is attempted, 4) a great point needs to be made."

I added lots of specifics of the crumbling marriage and my concerns for me and for my children. God was telling me, "I want a family," when I was sitting in church with two of my three family members. It made sense to me then. It still makes sense, although I go through bouts of impatience. I've filled my years with many lessons and distractions.

Physical affirmations manifested shortly after that message in church about family. My daughter had stitches in her finger from an accident in the park. The curious toddler kept taking the egg-shaped bandages off saying, "Look Mommy, a baby bird." She unwrapped it before we were a block from the emergency room. So, I stood on an aisle in Walgreens by Winter Park Hospital overwhelmed by choices for bandaging wounds. I concentrated on finding one she might leave intact. My two toddlers stood quietly with me. A soft raspy voice behind me said, "You have a lovely family." I turned and it was an elderly woman with a walker, hunched over barely able to speak. She continued, "God is blessing your family. I've been watching you with your children. I worked in child care all of my life. I know a strong family. God told me to tell you this."

Her daughter was my age and apologizing for her mother's interruption but said, "She insisted in talking to you. I couldn't stop her."

I assured both the intercessor and her daughter that the message was both received and appreciated.

Only the three of us stood there, no man. My perception of family was two adults, not one. My daughter's finger healed, and the woman's words helped heal my angst of divorcing. The words are soothing to my soul even in recollection from so many years past. The intercessor bandaged my broken heart.

In that same toddler and pre-school era, I was play-date buddies with another mother. She had gift of intercession. She had dabbled in New Age spiritual explorations as I was starting to do at the time, but she settled back into a traditional Christian belief. Wherever her wisdom came from, she was highly spiritual. My Christian friend said that I would come to know Jesus more deeply than she ... something I could not fathom with her deep dedication to her faith. She helped me interpret a dream. Again, it was just my children and I. We were in the desert. We were hiding in a tent and the scorching sand was blowing wildly outside. We were afraid. There was a thundering pounding and shaking of the ground and then a thud and then silence. In the vision, when I peeked outside, there was a mammoth stone male lion 30 feet high resting at the tent entrance. I shared with my friend the scary dream.

She interpreted the dream, "The lion was not there to trap you or deny you or scare you. That lion is God protecting you and your children. The fear will not get past your stone lion. Think of the lion as you make your way when you feel fear."

In my dictionary of dreams, a lion is a symbol of social distinction or business leadership. Wild animals in dreams are good omens for business depending upon their mood. I further interpreted the dream that I was safe to write.

My Christian friend knew when I needed her. This was before cell phones so telepathy was the communication method of the day. After my separation, I was visiting my first boyfriend in New Hampshire where he owned Bed and Breakfast inns. I was walking by myself up the mountain picking wild flowers while he made pancakes with Vermont maple syrup for his inn guests. I was lost in my activity. I was lost in my thoughts. I had gone for a two week visit without my children to determine if I or we could live there. The answer would ultimately be no. I stood up from my focus on the details of the tiny wildflowers. I turned and saw the expansive horizon of the whole White Mountain range. The contrast was shocking. Y told me in that moment, "Keep your expansive vision. You are a treasure." My Christian friend interceded within an hour. She said she felt she had to call me. She described a vision of a mountain range and she affirmed the exact words I had heard, "Keep your expansive vision. You are a treasure."

My Christian friend and her children moved from Florida. In years before e-mailing and instant messaging and texting, it was hard to stay in touch. Long distance calls used to have extra charges and fees, too. I did write letters, but primarily to family. I missed her dearly.

I wasn't regularly attending church. I would get my sermon messages from her on playgrounds in our conversations. I missed that, too. Two reasons for me for the absenteeism in church. First, the hypocrites were difficult to witness. Then the strong energy of people placing their needs into the space was distracting to me. I would leave services feeling burdened not uplifted.

At the same era, I read about missionary work through a community church I attended sporatically. I prayed about being a missionary with the church and going to maybe Caribbean islands.

As I prayed about it, Y answered, "You will not knock on one door at a time, but millions at once through words in the mass media. For your faithfulness, you will be rewarded for generations $20 at a time."

After that spiritual message in my mid-thirties, I often priced books at $20 each. I had pages and pages of ideas for books and films. It would take years before I could get them in print. My life was busy.

I had traded navy blue for baby blue at that time. I was primarily a mom. I worked during school hours and tried to be home in the afternoons. My career started during the three-martini lunch era. Data replaced cocktails in my early career. The technology wave took off right before I took time to raise my family. With a pending divorce, I had to re-invent myself. I would become proficient at reinvention as a professional communicator over the years. My skill set would follow budgets. I freelanced as a TV producer, a book writer, a media buyer, a public relations person, a graphic artist, and basically whatever a client or ad agency was hiring. When I was lucky, in spurts at a time, my skill set would also follow my heart.

Remembering this and reading the notes from the distant past, brought the events to life in my present. While my youthfulness was fading, my faith was not. My conviction to stay true to God's promise of a family was steadfast. The concept of forever love and family were deeply embedded desires driven deeper into my heart over the years. Time strengthened my faith, not diminished it. I clung to unwavering faith of the fulfillment of promises. I even started a book titled, "Rainbow Promises" as confirmation of my absolute resolve that my Twin Soul would manifest in this life. I waited to write it because I wanted the ending. If I was to encourage people and offer hope, I felt I needed to first be successful at achieving my own mission.

"Why would God voice this desire to me so specifically and then not deliver on His promise?" I asked and then answered out loud to myself, "Well, He will."

Every night that I was outside for decades, I would see a first star and place a wish to the heavens. I would say a childhood poem, "Star light, star bright, first star I see tonight, I wish I may, I wish I might, have the wish I wish tonight." Then I would simply wish for what was already specifically promised, "I want a family."

People manifest their own desires. For me, to manifest a spiritual promise had more logic. I peeked outside of my eastward facing window overlooking the ocean in Palm Beach, and twinkles of stars were appearing in the dusk. I started, "Star light ..."

# CHAPTER 13
## MEN DROPPING THE BALL

The unsightly bruise now in the twilight of the year 2015 was not going to cure for my New Year revelry regardless of my best intentions. I grew impatient, and stopped the healing and reading session to answer my iPhone.

"Bonne Annee! Bon jour le Chat," my Ted slurred in French, "Calling at sunset because I know you are allergic to dusk."

"Ha! Allergic to dust, or to dusk, I get it," I responded, "Sunset isn't my favorite time of day to be alone. Ann is supposed to be here but half hour late, not surprising. Having fun?"

"Warming up for the ball drop with some helicopter drops on the back slopes," he said.

"Make sure you don't come home in a cast because we have some casting of fishing rods to do next week," I said.

"Kisses," he said as I heard voices in the background get closer.

I heard a squeaky voice calling, "Teddy Bear. Apres Ski aqui."

"Teddy Bear, really? Eeeew," I grimaced to myself.

"That sounds like Eva. Is she there?" I asked already knowing the irritating voice was hers. He denied he even knew her. Sometimes he would forget he didn't know her and would say they were just friends.

"There are people all around, of course, but I'm here with Captain Ed and Dave," he said.

Dave was Eva spelled backwards. He would say he was talking to Dave on the phone, but I could hear a female voice. I couldn't deal with that reality now in this moment. I just wanted to get off the phone.

"Adios. Feliz Ano Nuevo," I said.

He responded in German with a growl, "Frohes Neues Jahr ... Kisses Cat."

No texts. I checked my e-mail. Owen and his wife sent sentimental holiday greetings from Paris. Owen confirmed that I would have a light work schedule for January. He was of the age of people who knew what a Smith Corona typewriter was, before self-correction. He preferred in order, meeting in person, a handwritten note. He tolerated e-mail and never texted. Neither did King Midas. The two reminded me of each other in many ways. Owen's wife was lucky. I'd like to be lucky, too. I hadn't yet chosen lucky.

J texted, "I passed on the NY gig for a better one later in Jan. No other news."

The Uber driver Armando picked us up and then he picked us up. He drove a shiny black 1999 3-Series BMW in mint perfect condition, just like him. He stayed with us for the evening. He was polite and funny and easy on the eyes.

As he drove us one mile to The Steak Out, he entertained the adoring Ann who couldn't stop staring at him, "So we are on South County now, which is called Palm Beach Avenue by Palm Beachers. We're heading to Royal Poinciana, which is called Main Street by the local Islanders. You know there are only three bridges, the North Bridge at Royal Poinciana, Middle Bridge at Royal Palm and the Southern Bridge is easy to remember, it's on Southern Boulevard."

"I've been building my driving business with the tourists by being a good tour guide," he bragged, "Yep, I started out as a lifeguard here. Now I've moved up to biz suits but I'm standing on the sidewalk. I'm preparing now for my entrepreneurial side to make me phat. My dad says I have to have a job so I have one to please him. I'm working on my real business on the side. Stay tuned sports fans!"

Armando didn't seem upset by his recent breakup. "Next!" is a common expression among single dating Pi-landers.

"My ex chose between honey and money, and she chose money. She's in St. Barths this week. My dad's there, too. She could have waited a few years for my inheritance and had both honey and money," he said matter-of-factly.

In the backseat, I whispered sarcastically to Ann, "Unless Miss Ex nabs the dad and spends it all before it's passed down. P.S. Rowboat."

Tennis Player joined us for the first round of champagne. He reminded me of a young Ted. He was immature. Ted and men from my era, were youthful but not immature like men in their thirties today. Armando and Tennis Player found surfing in common.

"The last tropical storm brought in five-footers," claimed Armando.

"The waves are shore breaks in Palm Beach. The ocean floor isn't conducive to creating surfable waves here. You have to surf further north in Florida for consistent waves and longer rides. And you want the waves to break further out, so you don't break your neck in shallow water," I added, sounding like a mother. I was a mother. I was a former competitive surfer. I felt too mature for these two. The fast friends made plans to go to The Steak Out in South Beach together.

They belonged there with leggy 20-somethings.

The lighted colored glass behind the shelf of liquor bottles cast a cool yellow tint the color of Veuve across our faces. The orange-ish light made Tennis Player look older. I could see the sun damage on his face. I could also see his adorable dimple and naturally pink lips as though he had a permanent makeup procedure. I was staring at him clicking a mental photograph. I planned to move him from the present into a memory. His veneered teeth were bleached very, very white shining almost neon in the orange hue. He kissed me on the cheek and excused himself to go meet his friends.

Ann found our reserved signs on the wood bar. It didn't feel celebratory that we were in a restaurant at a bar on a holiday. Although we were among many singles doing the same thing. It felt festive only because I was entertaining her.

"These are great seats right by the door. Good idea to dine at the bar to people watch," said Ann giving me credit for her idea.

Ann spotted a cast member of "Housewives" of somewhere. She spotted an aging rock star.

"I know some of the locals, but not the pop stars. I'm so busy creating pop culture that I rarely indulge in it. For me, it's a treat to watch TV or films or read recreationally," I said.

"I'm a pop-junkie," admitted Ann.

She pointed out an attractive woman making out with a shell-shocked preppy man with a pink jacket and noted it wasn't midnight.

"She oversells her sexuality. She's a likeable person. I don't know why she overwhelms men like that. She looks like a praying mantis hovering over him. Men think they will like aggressive women till they have someone mauling them in public. Watch that guy. Did you see him roll his eyes? Men instinctively like to be the hunters," I said.

"I'd like to kiss someone! This place looks interesting at first glance but in detail it looks like the gay '90s; the men look to be gay or in their 90s," deduced Ann.

"That can be an accurate observance at times here," I laughed.

A woman walked by and her face was swollen in a different manner than usual. Her lips were typically puffy with cosmetic injectibles, but this time it was around her eyes with an odd smooth indented area on her cheeks between the swollen facial features. She was wearing layers of mix-matched necklaces. She waved nervously. I protected her from backhand remarks by Ann and answered before Ann asked, "She's a high-end hoarder. Greed and materialism manifest in her in maniacal daily shopping sprees of consignment stores strewn with discarded designer wear. Other than her shopping obsession, she is good company. Because I know her, I understand her compulsive shopping is to fill a void in her created by great loss. Material possessions can't fill our hearts, but they can fill our time. The excess plastic surgery also is fueled by insecurity. She was age-appropriate pretty before she decided she didn't want wrinkles. I'll call and check on her later. She looked upset," I said.

"Hey-hey," waved a striking woman dressed to the nines with a small group of women.

"I can hear the subtle Southern accent. Who is that belle?" asked Ann.

"She actually isn't from the South but lived there a long time. She's here now. I think she uses the Southern drawl to try to stand out among the throngs of beautiful women. I don't have the accent but I'm actually named Charlotte because my mother's family settled the South including City Council Members of Charlotte and one of the first governors of North Carolina. My mother was an actress headed to Broadway so she didn't have an accent," I said.

"I forget that about your family. I just always think of you being Floridian and being my friend," said Ann.

"Because it's always about you," I laughed, actually really meaning that she was a bit self-absorbed.

"I'm having people over tomorrow if you want to stop by," offered an alluring woman holding hands with a buff stud both in tiny tight clothes, who didn't wait for an answer.

Ann asked, "So, her?"

"She is from a former-mob family. She was a good friend to me after the Unlucky 13 cyber stalking era. She knew how to have your back. It's uncanny how a mutual bond was formed instantly with us. She had a stalker situation, too. You almost have to experience the intensity first-hand to understand the severity of the traumatic bullying. She has natural beauty. She is all real, no plastic surgery. She internet dates and the guys go crazy over her. She is ten years older than us, but you would never think that by her looks. I'm not sure internet dating gets the desired results based on the research of her many dates," I explained.

"So, what is up with that woman staring at us?" Ann asked.

"Well, you missed it, but on the way in her date gave you a long look. If a man pays attention to you for one minute, the date will check you out for one hour to try to find your flaws to point out to the man. Women aren't big on being sincere friends with other women in a competitive superficial scene," I explained.

"Love you Cat! So, what is your name? Let's be Facebook friends," a loud character with a wide fake grin rambled her speel to Ann uncomfortably close to her face. She was reinventing herself in a new career, looking for a husband, and was obnoxious in her overzealous need to feel accepted by anyone and everyone.

She added her new social media friend to her score in the pretend online popularity contest then darted away.

I shared, "She's an energy vampire. Also, I have learned to be cautious of the people who right out of the box 'love you' and put 'xo' on texts before they know you. They tend to be the first to slap that x as a target on your back. Love and hugs and kisses in a normal world are earned by human interaction in the physical world, not in the imaginary online world."

I added, "Also, I am a Capricorn. By our nature we are reserved and cautious. You won't find a more loyal friend, but we take our time in letting you get close. In my next life I want to be a Sagittarius like you. I want to be the impulsive free-spirited flirty friend!"

"I got Armando's dad's birthday, so I want to look up our compatibility in your Zodiac birthday book," Ann added to the topic of Astrology.

A small group came in and mingled around us. They were meeting for a drink then taking the Brightline fast train to Miami for the evening. They were some of my favorite people. They were who they said they were and they didn't have any apparent agendas. They were more like me in that we believed we were each interesting enough so we didn't have to talk about other people to carry on a conversation. I enjoyed my time with them when I joined their group or met them individually.

Ann, on the other hand, was very interesting. She was also interested in other people's business much more than I ever was. Maybe because I'm a ghostwriter and the keeper and controlled teller of people's secrets, that I see details of people's lives as my career, not my leisure activity.

"Hey, what is that plastic face barking at you?" Ann whispered.

A rail-thin tall peroxide blonde with fire truck red lips poked me repeatedly on the shoulder from behind, "Hello. Hello. Didn't you see me?"

Her awkward entourage of four young adults stood sentry stiff and quiet.

"I'm just on the Island for a few days before I jet off to Cannes and New York again. We must do lunch but I've just been so darn busy," she gloated with her plastic surgeon crafted nose upturned.

"We're getting our party fare from Amici's Market for our pool-side party. I'm just here for a quick martini and to pick up some appetizers," she chirped.

I noticed she said I when she was with a group, so grammatically she could have said we. She is a me, not we kind of gal. She didn't ask about my life. She didn't introduce herself to Ann, or for that matter, even look at Ann after the initial jealous glance of her curvy body. The Alpha was flat-chested. The drones marched off like baby ducks behind their mentor.

"That is funny that you said 'bark' because she calls herself the Alpha Dog of Palm Beach. I am not much of a dog person, but Alpha must mean 'Alone.' I see her primarily with her 'sheeple' or her unaware sheep-like paid people. Occasionally she attracts a potential friend but people don't want to be treated like dog food. She's rather mean spirited. She is all about herself. She's the definition of narcissist," I inadvertently slipped into catty Ann mode.

"Her affected group oozes her arrogance and self-importance. She looks like a classic whippet-thin bunny boiler to me," quipped Ann.

"Ha! 'Fatal Attraction' film! Look, we don't sound much better than her. Listen to us. She can't help herself. She is nuevo riche. My mother always said, 'You can't learn how to have class, you have to be born with it.' This one bought her way in with a giant mortgage into a zip code she can barely afford, with a down payment from a lucrative divorce. She can't buy class. What makes being around her uncomfortable is that she's trying too hard to show off her material life and doesn't connect with people on a human to human level. She doesn't want anyone to know about her past. If you are mean, people won't warm up to you and you then don't have to explain your past. People call her The Mean Girl. I don't like talking about people negatively. It makes me feel bad inside. Everyone has faults," I explained my uneasiness.

"It's great people watching here. While I'm looking I try to look for positives. Palm Beach in large part is a mix of irreverence, decadence, and luxury in a small space of an island with only 10,000 residents in high season. Everything and everyone are bigger than life here.

The types of characters are likely in many communities but they are more exaggerated here. Observing the frailty of human nature is easy here because people wear their insecurities and vulnerabilities on top like a Hermes scarf. Maybe it is the healer in me that I can see it so clearly. The more they try to overcompensate for what they feel are inadequacies, the more their actions and behaviors point out what they try to obscure. There is a lot of pressure on Pi-landers to be rich and social and beautiful. That creates a lot of angst on a person's insides to uphold to that high standard in so many areas of life for years on end. Then you add the devastating gossip. If you don't have an apparent blaring fault, you get assigned one. Some of the people have too much time on their hands. Gossip is the hobby of the bored and the boring. Gossip is for those that feel out of control in their own lives, so they shift negativity to others. That's another topic," I suggested.

The barrage of questions about the cast of characters was exhausting to me. I entertained my guest and friend. I assumed if we were noticed, we would be summarized in a phrase or sentence, too. Nobody is a string of a just dozen words. We were in my opinion more likely to be lost in the glamor, glitz and grandeur of the oncoming crowd.

# CHAPTER 14
# WORDS MATTER

I brushed through the crowd in the sitting area towards the ladies' room and a friend stopped me. He pulled a small white paper folded note from his wallet and discreetly flashed it to me. I had given the note to him a few years ago when he had health issues.

"I've kept this note with me. I have read this many times, and for many reasons. Because you believed, you made me believe, and it's made a difference in my life. I have life. I'm alive. Let's start there," and he expressed his gratitude with tears building.

He opened his palm and looked down and I read the note in blue ink in my handwriting that said, "Believe in a Miracle."

This substantive exchange in the sea of superficiality energized me. Everything has purpose and is in the Universe's perfect timing. He reminded me to Believe in a Miracle.

I walked back to Ann and she inquired, "So who is that good looking age-appropriate man?"

"He is a very important friend in my life. We wrote a few important words together," I summarized as the buzz in the room made it harder to talk.

# CHAPTER 15
## GROUND ZERO FOR SIZE ZERO

Size-zero beautiful bartenders in micro-mini skirts flitted behind the bar.

Ann ordered for us laughing with the bartender, “She and I will split the small filet, cooked medium. We’ll split the Cesar salad. No potatoes. I really want the giant crab claws there at the seafood bar, but I’ll skip those calories because I want to be a skinny-bitch like you.”

“The crab claws are flown in from The Keys daily. You should try them,” she sold and added, “I’ve worked every night this holiday. This skinny body hasn’t had a full meal or a good night’s sleep in a week and I hurt all over.”

Armando ordered crab claws, insisting that we share and worry about calories later. He ordered more than three people could possibly eat. He ordered another bottle of Veuve Clicquot Yellow Label. He handed the bartender a black American Express credit card with his father’s name on it.

“Most of these people are couples. Where are the singles?” asked Ann.

“Some of them are single, they are just on dates. Remember when we were in Naples for New Year’s and there was the nervous online dating first-date couple at Campiello’s?” I asked.

“That was so bizarre. The girl was so intoxicated and was asking her date if he was ready to get naked.They just met,” she said.

“Remember then, all the so-called couples at the bar said they were with dates they met through online dating sites. Guys take the easy way out these days rather than finding love in a romantic way,” I said.

“I know you are waiting for your divine intervention to bring Prince Charming or Harrison Gore, but you really should try online dating sometime. Help the Universe out a little! It’s a great ego boost to get all the fab feedback. It’s so easy, I can show you. It takes a lot of hours to sort through all the responses. I know you are busy, so I thought about setting up a profile for you,” Ann said.

“That is so wrong! The internet is not an option for dating after being cyber stalked. Anyway, I’m not a hopeless romantic. I am a hopeful romantic. I believe in love,” I stated.

“Just like online, sorting candidates in person has challenges since I, like many other people, am here in Palm Beach just part time. It’s the ultimate adult playground. You see people here when they are having fun. It takes extreme time and effort to really know someone," I said.

"I see men now who I dated a decade ago when I was dating older men, 'older' being sixty. They could have had anyone. They chose instead everyone. Now they have no-one. Notice the debonair silver haired man in the corner seat. Today he's here with a stunning Russian-rent-a-date. Sometimes they marry them," I added.

"The Russian women you see walking their tiny pampered dogs on leashes during the day and at night their men follow them around like puppies. Look at that guy. He's glassy-eyed thinking, 'She likes me!' Ted says highly trained KGB operatives work here. They use the same techniques in catching a husband as they do in spying: beauty, intelligence and aggression, their tools of the trade," I said.

"Who's the Mr. Focker next to him? I'm watching you," she laughed and pointed her two fingers at her eyes and then at me like the dad in "Meet the Fockers" movie.

"Another one, he's the guy who put the roofie in my drink. I ended up in his guest room on a twin bed with all of my clothes on in the morning and bolted out of there before coffee. His antics didn't work with me, even drugged! I never understood why. It was our fourth date and I had agreed to stay at his house. I potentially liked him till he tried to pull that Cosby stunt," I said.

"Then I got set up with the Palm Beach Gardens con man who had a rap sheet a mile long and fresh out of federal prison. He left town with Rolexes and cash of people who befriended him," I said.

"That was a scary character," she exclaimed.

"Then there are the married or committed men. They forget to mention that till the third date," I shrugged.

"Last week, I found the box of self-help books you gave me from the 'Venus – Mars' era, around the time I separated over 20 years ago. Titles like 'If the Buddha Dated,' 'How Not to Stay Single Past 40,' etcetera. The pages have yellowed but I still plan to read them one day," I said.

"You didn't have time to read them then because you were too busy dating!" she laughed.

"I was flirty, footloose and fancy free. Now I'm 50. I plan to marry and adore someone for 30 or 40 years. Not just anyone, but Harrison Gore. I wish Ted was my forever. I do love him so. Finding my twin soul has been an arduous process. Sometimes I feel like it's like I'm getting a stock tip to a Ponzi scheme, and get in after all the other investors just to fund their profits. I've set up a lot of couples. I'm a good matchmaker," I said and waved to a couple as they walked in that I introduced to each other.

"What?" she asked over the music increasing greatly in volume.

The D.J. house music started at 9 p.m. in the seating area. Armando grabbed Ann's hand and whisked her to the makeshift dance floor in the living-room style seating area of white leather bucket chairs and coffee tables. Armando had good rhythm. I've always speculated that people are intimate in the same manner they dance. Armando was very likely proficient at both. I unenthusiastically danced with a guy friend.

Fireworks marked midnight. The privately funded display burst over the intercoastal waterway behind Flagler Museum's exclusive historical Coconuts party. We were going to stop by that party and a party at the Biltmore, but parties were in full motion and friends at the parties weren't texting back. I was ready to go home anyway. We walked outside and down the sidewalk with the fireworks bursting next to us over the waterway.

Texts came in from Ted and Tennis Player, which could be interchangeable.

The in-person Tennis Player was wooing a circle of post-collegiate looking tipsy beauties. I could see him behind me on the sidewalk in front of the restaurant. His text message conflicted with his actions. He bored and bothered me. Ted had a decade of dedication, so I dismissed hunches of infidelity at times. In the case of Tennis Player, I was more interested in the fireworks. I watched the flamboyant display of pyrotechnics, to rival any Disney fireworks display.

After the finale, we got in Armando's BMW and drove to the Chesterfield Hotel. Ann and Armando stayed downstairs at the Leopard Lounge. A lively five-piece band had couples from 40 to 90-years-old pulsating on the dance floor. I went up to Ann's suite and fell asleep on the sofa. I didn't want to go home by myself. It had been a long New Year's Eve. Even surrounded by people, it was long and lonely.

I woke pre-sunrise in my dress. Ann had made it to her bed. I tiptoed barefoot out of the room to my place.

I moved my all-time favorite book "Seventeen Ways to Eat a Mango" from a shelf to the southwest corner of the small apartment on the kitchen counter. Feng Shui principles suggest to bring good energy to strengthen your love life, start in the southwest corner. This yin or feminine energy of the home strengthens the role of the woman to create harmony in love. It made sense to me. In order to be happy in love, I must first be happy within myself.

The book is about a canning executive who goes to a remote island to prepare for a corporate fruit canning company to occupy the island and instead he gets indoctrinated to island life. He went back to basics. My life somehow had gotten more complicated than I wished. The book had been out of print for some years. I ordered used ones online for gifts. This was one of the used books. A business card fell out of the book. I picked it up and it read, "Jeremiah 29:11 "For I know the plans I have for you," declares the LORD, "plans to prosper you and not to harm you, plans to give you hope and a future."

I placed the book and the card eye level. Things have energy. This combo certainly had positive energy for me.

# CHAPTER 16
# THE TAME GAME

I changed into a swimsuit while the radio sang a song by Natasha Bedingfield, "I've got a pocket, a pocket full of sunshine ... I smile up to the sky, I know I'll be alright ..."

I could hear vicious waves striking the shore. I thought I heard rain, but it was palm leaves rhythmically whipping against my window.

As the sun rose, I greeted 2016 with a quick beach walk. After being stalked, I made a habit of absolutely no habits. I was unpredictable. I would randomly alternate biking on the bike trail, walking along Worth or the beach. I took different routes. Today I walked to the northern entrance to the public beach.

A brown duck hiding in tall grasses by the sidewalk quacked.

"He is quite out of place. He's not hiding well as he's making too much noise," I thought.

The black sky spit sprays of rain. Gusts threw my visor into the sand. The sand singed my corneas so I faced the offshore oncoming storm, the sand bullets bounced off of my new scratch-free sunglasses. A thick 75 degree humid bubble of oxygen filled my lungs.

The storm washed up man-o-wars into the brown seaweed. The purple bubble bodies had tentacles 24 inch long. The tentacles could sneak up and poison you, like you stare at obvious evidence of a cyber stalker, and he's busy stealing your data in another portal.

A single seagull fought the gusty winds 10 feet over the choppy waves. He dropped down to catch a long skinny needle fish. I wondered how he could see the fish in the churned-up waters.

I considered maybe I should leave the haunted backpack contents and my Palm Beach history behind and stay in Owen's New York condo for the rest of January.

"Birds fish in windy weather," said Y.

I agreed that perseverance and tenacity were admirable traits, but the island life felt smothering today.

The high tide was crashing into the 20 foot seawall to the south. The water was unusually high.

I turned back to exit the beach. I was surprised to see the 7 a.m. swimmers gathering. A group meets daily at Australian Avenue with snorkels and masks for a several mile ocean swim. I had planned to join them when I moved to Palm Beach. I had been captain of my swim team, a synchronized swimmer, and a competitive surfer. I loved water sports. The swimmers were all men, and somehow that made me not join them. I felt I was athletic enough to swim with them whether they were men, women, mammals, marlins, turtles or whatever. I could but I didn't.

I retreated to the eight block sidewalk on Ocean Boulevard. I bounced back and forth staying close to my place so I could dart inside when the oncoming wall of rain water over the horizon hit shore. The pellets of stinging rain hit and I darted inside to shower and pack.

There was a knock on the door. I don't have a peephole, so inquired who it was.

Tennis Player said, "Me," and continued as I let him in. "I left my keys with the Buccan valet ... Is it alright if I stay here till five when they open?"

"Sure," I cut him off. He smelled like chlorine. He was damp from pool water, not rain.

I was reminded of Y's message, "You cannot tame that which is wild."

I continued packing. Tennis Player tossed his damp clothes on the floor and sprawled out face-down naked across my queen-size bed. He snored in short order. Ted didn't snore.

His iPhone was facing up beside him on the bed. In the small space, I couldn't help but to see an incoming text with a selfie of a bare-breasted college-looking girl giving a 'come hither' look, and a text, "where r u? skinny dip n mimosas."

I thought to myself that the fact that I think "come hither" to describe her, placed us in very different generations.

I left with my luggage and my dignity. He was too young and too wild. He was not for me. In my mind, I renamed him simply "Player" not "Tennis Player." I had played the tame game with a few past boyfriends. The players can be a challenge and generally give entertainment for a few years at a stretch. At this time, I was neither in a space to tame or for game.

I stopped by the boat to drop off the radio. With sounds the boat might seem occupied. We hadn't hooked up cable at this marina and Captain Ed needed to fix the stereo. I peeked at the storage under the stair and the mystery iPhone was intact. I turned on a light in the galley and triple checked that I locked the door behind me.

J met me at Ta-boo when it opened at 11:30 a.m. We sat on the zebra fabric bar stools closest to the door. In that primo spot, you can see everyone in the sunny front dining room, everyone at the elongated bar, and the people who quietly pass to the more private back dining rooms.

A 40-something couple passed by in couture matching tangerine-colored outfits. Their dad likely covered their credit card bills. "Town and Country" likely covered their wedding. They were followed by a 80-something version of the same couple in royal blue.

"Palm Beach, where the gorgeous morph to geriatric in the confines of coastal condos and castles..." I noted.

"I'm hanging with the gorgeous crowd as long as I can hang," said J.

I ordered "the usual." Service was quick since we were the first seating. My water with extra lemon and Worth Avenue Salad appeared.

"This is heaven! Crab claws, shrimp, avocado, cherry tomato halves, capers, bib lettuce in a Dijon vinaigrette ... I could eat this every day," I purred.

"You do order that every day! It's annoying! Why don't you order something else?" bellowed J.

"I order different things at different places. This is what I order for lunch at Ta-boo," I responded.

"I'm the only person at lunch here who orders water. Most order a pomegranate martini or some other specialty cocktail and a menu item with at least three special requests. I keep my orders simple. I'm a simple person in general," I remarked.

We were unusually quiet as we dined.

A shopping-weary husband darted in for a lightning round.

He barked, "Rum and Coke stat. Here's a $50 and I'll have it finished by the time you make another. If I'm paying double in these stores I may as well be seeing double," he said.

He gulped his coping medicine and wrestled with an armload of Max Mara and St. John bags to find his pocket for the change.

We could hear Pi-landers reminiscing next to us, "Ta-boo was two doors down back during the era when the Kennedys made Cirrhosis-by-the-Sea fun."

"It used to be 'Ta-boo or to-bed after dinner' and 'In bed by ten and home by one.' Thirty years ago, we danced here till three in the morning. We woke up to Bloody Mary drinks around ten, then came here for lunch with vodka and grapefruit. That was the big drink of the day. That end of the bar was cirrhosis corner because all those guys are dead now. Boy, were they fun, especially Martin," chuckled the impeccably dressed bow-tie suited 80-something man to our right.

His friend added, "You know how he lost his fortune? He spent half on wine, women and gambling and he wasted the other half."

The old-guys told another joke, "So, you know about the new guy who came into town. He dressed a little off but he was tan and buff. He sat between three of the widows and they started to grill him. 'We haven't noticed you around here,' one said. 'I've been in prison for 30 years. I just got out,' he responded. 'What were you in for?' she asked. 'For murdering my wife,' he answered. 'Well, fantastic, you're single,' she exclaimed," and the story-teller belly laughed at his own joke.

Right on cue, a newbie came barreling up to us, and condescendingly remarked to me, "I see you're ordering the same thing again. You don't experiment with the menu. You just aren't a foodie like I am."

Not that I wanted to engage the prickly remark but I asked anyway, "So, you are a foodie?"

"I've tried everything on the menu," she gave an illogical response as she pretended to talk to us as she scouted the talent in the room with her darting eyes.

"Well, I'm writing an article now on some European classics juxtaposed to new cuisine. Maybe you can help me decide which I should put in the feature. I'm thinking from my last trip Agape Substance in Rive Gauche. Then maybe the newly renovated Ritz in Place Vendome or Laurent on Champs Elysees or Le Bristol's Epicure. Le Cinq is divine but everyone would know to go to the Four Seasons. For daytime Mini Palais is the clear winner for this article, or maybe the Costes L'Avenue. Well, I've narrowed down those for Paris. For London I love the Connaught's Helene Darroze and the Champagne Room is spectacular ...," I rattled off at rapid-fire speed.

I normally can't recall names of people, places or venues on demand, so I was pretty amazed myself.

The 50-ish recently divorced redhead's eyes had glazed over. She made a loud sigh. She had no comment. She'd been trolling around at lunchtime the last few weeks to check for the next credit card-wielding Mr. Right. She grilled J with a few pointed questions.

The divorcee bored with J in short order and pretended she saw someone in the back dining room. She excused herself, took her time sauntering past the white-haired men, and the hour-glass silhouette disappeared between the white linen-topped tables and out of the back door.

J said, "Wow Cat, you're usually more understated in your bimbo meter. That was harsh for you."

"We're never in our most gracious state when feeling extreme stress. My snarkiness did not seem to phase her. She isn't focused on me or what I think," I said.

"She did have some thick skin and she had a pretty big shovel for that gold-digging, too. She was trying to hide it but the handle was sticking out of her bag. These guys grew up chasing ballerinas. Then models were in vogue for arm candy. That one was neither category. She's so full of shit. I tell all of my friends both male and female when they start dating someone to hint of financial woes and see if the potential romantic mate sticks around. It's a good test," he remarked.

We turned our attention back to our own conversation.

"So, you are intuitive. How about you give me a quick reading to start my new year?" asked J.

"I'm not a magician or a jester. I only get, and certainly only give, intuitive insights when I am directed by Spirit. I've reluctantly done it a few times with disastrous results," I said.

"So, your readings weren't true?" he asked.

"No, truth is truth. Most people don't really want truth. Here is an example. I met a guy for drinks after my divorce. We were getting to know each other and I mentioned something about his adopted son. He got enraged. He wanted to know who told me. He spilled that his wife seduced him without protection, got pregnant, and they had to move up the wedding. The baby wasn't his. The woman tricked him. I knew. He didn't want proof of what he already knew inside. Then another time in Palm Beach, a woman begged me to help give her hope for her love life. I did. What showed up energetically was an old boyfriend which I described to her. She got so hysterical crying and said she wanted to commit suicide except she wanted to stay alive for her dog. It's not my job to give people truths that they don't want to hear. I like to teach people to connect to their own truths directly from the source," I said.

"Hey, let's talk strategy of communication," I changed the subject.

I showed J a pair of flip phones from Unlucky 13. I gave him one and kept one.

"These are throw-away phones. We just pay by the minute. You have plenty of minutes left on this one. If it gets low, just go to Verizon, and load more minutes. It's easy. Communicate by text but if need be, we have this as back up for private communications," I said, pushing the phone into his hand.

"Sunshine, why do I need this?" he asked.

"Hopefully you don't. Here is an extra key to the boat. Go by the marina and turn on different lights each day and make sure it's locked. If you need to contact me in private regarding The Project, contact me on this phone only," I instructed.

J fidgeted as we whispered our agendas for the next few weeks, "I'm picking up Ted now at the Palm Beach Airport. We'll drive to Miami, fly to Costa Rica, fly back to Miami, drive to Key West, then we drive back north, I'll drop him off in Fort Lauderdale, and I'll drive back here to Palm Beach."

I headed to the airport to pick up Ted over the Southern Bridge. The storm had already passed as storms typically do in Florida. The Pi-landers drove on the 20 mile-per-hour stretch of Ocean Boulevard with their car tops down. I opened my convertible top to a gray but dry sky.

Ann had put on a 1970s station on the radio, and The Carpenters from "California Dreamin'" harmonized, "All the leaves are brown and the sky is gray ..."

When I was married, a neighbor would sing this song to me every time he saw me. He said I was uniquely mellow and content like a hippie contrasted to the other stay-at-home moms in the affluent yuppie neighborhood. That seemed a lifetime ago. Thankfully I packed my lava-lamp contentment and optimism to take to my new life. At times, I've survived on oxygen and optimism.

Ted waved animatedly as I pulled into the small private executive airport. He tossed his bulging Orvis suitcase over the back and it took up the whole backseat with all ski clothes.

He planted a big welcome kiss on me and exclaimed, "Boy, I had a wild time in Aspen with Ed!"

I smiled and said simply, "Interesting choice of words," and thought, "You cannot tame that which is wild."

# CHAPTER 17
## COSTA RICA BOUND

We drove to Ted's Fort Lauderdale penthouse to trade his ski clothes for pre-packed beach, fishing and resort wear. Ted entertained me with tales of the St. Regis. He reminded me of our romantic trip to Aspen St. Regis, and how we also dined at Little Nell and the Jerome. He was the master conversationalist. He turned my images of guy trip to our previously shared romantic trip. I did love him, both then and now. I knew I was being manipulated. His charms worked to calm me and make me feel loved and protected in the moment.

"I see you've been healing yourself again," he mentioned and pointed to my bruised shin with white finger imprints.

"I had a spill because of that bully troll curly tail lizard on the second step," I laughed.

When he was with me, Ted was very attentive.

"You are wearing your dragonfly necklace. That looks stunning on you. I got that for you in Park City. We went there to go to Sundance Film Festival, and we had so much fun skiing on the empty slopes, we never made it to the film festival events," he recalled.

"I love this necklace. The dragonfly represents the Cross of Lorraine. The wings look like the double cross of the Crusader's cross symbol. Joan of Arc carried the Cross of Lorraine with her to war, as did the Knights Templar in the Crusades. It makes me feel protected," I said.

"You are protected by your necklace and by me. You have a spiritual answer for every detail of your life," he commented.

"Every detail of my life is spiritual," I smiled.

We stayed at Ted's and caught the first two hour flight from Miami to San Jose, Costa Rica. We traded in $100 for 46,475 colones which we called "monkeys."

"So, a dollar is about 500 of these monkeys. Don't let me leave a $300 tip like I did in Uruguay at lunch! Let's move our watches back one hour for the time change here. And make a note for us to rent from Hertz at the airport and not wait for the Avis bus next time," he noted as he paced back and forth on the sidewalk outside of the airport.

I adjusted my watch. It was 11:11. I was scribbling notes in my notebook for my upcoming book. The journalist in me, keeps a blue ink pen busy when I'm not reeling in fish or holding onto bike handle bars or holding Ted's hand.

"Look at the gun guard stands at every parking lot. Bahamian rustic is 'cute' because of the Easter egg colors. This place is painted in muted sun-faded autumn tones, not my favorite. Check out this barb wire décor, too!" I noted.

"Remember Owen was telling us about how homes will become fortresses internationally? Bougainvillea thorns are a natural theft deterrent like we see in the Mediterranean. Remember large hedges in the Dominican, too? Decorative wrought iron can work. Barbed wire here, and in Peru and other places we've been says, 'stay out!' Costa Ricans don't mess around. They have the least amount of police per population in the world. The criminal system here is barbaric. You get your hand cut off for hocking a $100 ring," he said.

I winced at the visual and added, "Crime isn't a poor civilization's problem. Even on Palm Beach Island crime is up. Pi-landers say the robberies are by the trusted lawn crews and cleaning people."

In the grungy Porto Novo neighborhood by the rental car lot, the Avis attendant recommended a local joint for a quick lunch. The beef barbeque nachos could have fed a family and Ted claimed the chicken cordon bleu to be world-class. He liked that lunch was $10 including tips. We paid with a handful of colones and left as the locals started streaming into the open-air picnic style hospital-clean shack.

As we drove, Ted noted, "Notice the polite traffic patterns. Motorcycles have just one or two passengers and not an entire family like the Dominican Republic. Also, there is some litter but nothing like the Dominican."

If anything, Ted was speeding as we guided the rental car towards our fishing spot, Los Suenos.

"The guys were in a tournament last week and said the sailfish are smokin'," said Ted.

"I'd put you on a fishing team over most men I know. You are stronger, surprising, but true. I've watched you fishing, snorkeling, hiking, skiing, biking, or anything athletic. You have the endurance. You won't stop. And you have razor sharp focus. I've never heard you whine. Even most men whine and complain when the fishing gets rigorous. You just talk to the fish and tell him to give up and yank them in the boat," Ted complimented me.

"Then why can't I fish in the tournaments? You tell me how good I am and I prove you right," I asked.

"Because you are a girl," he said shrugging his shoulders.

I got quiet. I had learned not to argue with him. He would win, or more precisely, we would both lose.

"The senoritas at the Marlin Club in San Jose strut around serving shots. Many guys stop in there before heading to the marina. Prostitution is de facto legal here. It's not uncommon for underage girls to be at the club," he made conversation.

"I don't need to know that detail of guy trip to Costa Rica. Nor do I need to know about the Cuban teenagers, or Blacks Club in Buenos Aires by the Alvear Palace, or any of the other places," I huffed.

"Blacks is so cool. Even U.S. politicians get busted there. Remember the politician who had the beautiful South American girlfriend? Now, you know I don't go to those places. You should be aware of what is around you as a writer. It makes you more interesting. Life is interesting. You don't have to agree with it to know it exists," he said.

"I am a writer. We are best friends. Sometimes you forget that I am also the girlfriend. Talk of hooker girls does not seem appropriate conversation for a romantic trip," I responded.

Antiquated low hanging electric wires lined the two-lane Costa Rica 27 Road. Siri's GPS voice guided us by rustic un-air-conditioned open fruit stands, plant nurseries and tire stores. I wondered what the hard-working light brown skinned men carrying rakes and shovels on their shoulders, walking along from field to field, thought about their young family members serving shots at the Marlin Club.

An hour into the drive, the interstate turned hilly and green with vegetation. The road cut through small clay hills. Fields were framed with raw logs, actual trees and wire.

"Look a billboard, 'Los Suenos 45 minutes away,'" I read breaking the silence as we approached bigger hills then small mountains of the jungle ahead.

"Los Suenos is about ten degrees warmer than where we are in South Florida. They don't have hurricanes or earthquakes here.

We went through a few tolls where our paper monkey money was exchanged for giant metal coins worth nearly nothing. A guy was selling cut mangoes to the stopped cars in the toll lane.

"See the brown grass fields and scraggly trees and dry wild banana trees? They won't stay that dry. When the rains hit, that is what all the drains on the side of the roads are for, it monsoons," he said.

"You're more likely to die of a falling rock from these ancient volcanic mountains than a car accident. They don't tolerate speeding here. See all the Parque Nacional?" he noted.

"Hey, I forgot my Spanish dictionary," I said digging around in my purse, "Remember when we practiced all the way to Buenos Aires? You didn't know when we would use 'gato' in conversation then there were all the stray cats in the winery?"

"And remember when we went all over the Domincan asking about 'bagua' because you wanted a purse, a bag, and finally as Casa de Campo they told us we were asking for a bug?" he laughed.

"And in Paris, I first used my iTranslate app at George Cinc, and he said my own French was better than the iTranslate which ordered fine toilet water, not fine French wine," I chuckled.

"Ah, farmlands, I'm recalling the Loire Valley and a Cat in a sunflower field like a Van Gogh painting. I wish you didn't erase those photos," reminisced Ted.

"I kept the ones that were not as risqué. The Sancerre wines got to our better judgement among the sunflowers," I said.

Our spirits were brighter than the blight we passed.

"These sparse farm houses and fruit stands are fabricated like our tool sheds in the U.S. We have it so good as U.S. citizens," I remarked.

We passed occasional fruit stands with neat rows of primary colored spheres of produce. The bright red, green and yellow added a welcome splash of color to the dreary scenery. The sun reflected off the metal corrugated roofs of the buildings. The road was dotted with large outdoor covered porches with picnic tables for social venues for the locals. The rustic gathering places didn't look welcoming to me. I gave thanks in my mind for my American upbringing. I was grateful for my American life.

At the third toll, we gave five of the huge gold coins. We made a turn and passed by pastures of thin Brahman cows with big back bumps as the mountains grew taller before us.

"We're now on Costa Rica Road 34 toward Jaco. It's the surfer mecca of the Pacific. With your surfer-girl self, you will love it. Well, except, it's covered in volcanic ash dusty dirt, not the white sugar sand that you like," Ted said being the consummate tour guide.

We passed a father and young son in overalls walking along the winding road.

The visual reminded me of my young son.

"When my son was three, I was contemplating the future of my family. My young son for several months gave me morning reports of the crops from 'The Farmer.' The analogies answered my questions about our future with exact precision. He gave words of encouragement of my future with instructions for tilling, pruning, fertilizing, and predictions of crops and weather patterns. I asked him to describe the farmer. As I sat with him on his playroom floor, he built his Lego masterpiece and described a grandfather looking gentleman farmer man with a hat. I asked if the farmer was speaking to him in his dreams and he told me yes. The younger children are, and the closer they are still to heaven, the easier it is to access heavenly hints for guidance. Some advisors say children can remember past lives until about age five. The farmer gave me solid advice and encouragement through intercession through my little earth-bound angel child," I chattered to Ted.

I hear a "ding" and pull out my iPhone. I had forgotten to turn it off after I checked messages at the airport. In international travel, I keep my phone off most of the time to avoid expensive roaming charges.

Ann texted me, "Wild time I see? Not invited?"

That "wild" word again, I noted to myself and texted back, "What?"

"Stopped by your place to stay here. My date's not coming now for a few more days. Door unlocked, empty champagne bottles, cigarette butts, even a bong ... you?" she texted.

"Bong? Then you know not me ... Tennis game over. Simply Player, not Tennis Player. I'm done," I clicked back.

"OK, I'll pick up this place for you. We can talk when you get back. Xo," she responded.

"Tks," I texted and turned off my iPhone.

"Everything OK in your Pi-lander world?" Ted asked.

"Sure. Ann is in a little mess. She is staying at my place in Palm Beach," I responded with my half-truth.

On the radio, Jim Croche crooned from the seventies, "Operator, can you disconnect this call... there's no one there I really wanted to talk to ..."

# CHAPTER 18
# LOST IN TIME AT VILLA CALETAS

We pulled up the steep one-lane long cobble stone driveway to Villa Caletas, a five-star hotel in the Central Pacific area. A half-mile hedge of red hibiscus plants separated our rental car from a steep drop off to the thick jungle below. A hunched uniformed worker was gingerly plucking red blooms and putting them in a basket hanging from his elbow. We barely had space to pass him. The road was narrow.

We checked into our villa, which had an incredible view of the mountainous jungle below. An active wasp nest kept us from exploring the private Jacuzzi on the deck. The attendant said he would take care of the stinging insects. On the deck, I pointed out the Jurassic Park size grasshopper.

"That's nothing Cat, check out this baby scorpion in the tub. He's just a little guy," he said as he lifted it with a piece of paper and flushed it.

"If there is a baby, there is a mama!" I squealed.

"You are in the jungle. It's safe. I've been here a lot with the boys," he reassured.

We left to dip into the endless pool overlooking Los Suenos marina on the Pacific coastline below.

"Because we are 15 degrees from the equator, there are 12 hours of light and 12 of day nearly year-round. Sunrise is around 6 a.m. so it will get dark here soon," he noted as we chose lounge chairs with a stunning view.

I read the cocktail menu and asked, "Is the ice here safe?"

"Yes, after World War II, Costa Rica disbanded the military and invested in infrastructure and education. It has the highest literacy rate between the U.S. and Brazil," Ted offered.

"Let's order the mango margaritas made from the mango grove just a mile from here," I suggested.

"Pure Vida!" he exclaimed as the orange frothy libations were delivered.

We watched sunset at 5:30 p.m. at the hotel's amphitheater next to the pool. We asked for the mango margaritas to be made with Grey Goose vodka. We named them Man-Goose. Ted was fun.

We had a reasonable dinner at the hotel's restaurant. A 2 foot-long brown iguana perched next to us on the outside deck dining room. We pointed out to the server a thick spider web with a leggy red-bodied spider in the middle in the plant beside us. He said nature lovers come to the jungle to witness such works of nature, and he swept the part of the web that was touching my chair with a napkin. We agreed the menu had limited choices of seafood for being in such close proximity to world-class fishing. They only offered shrimp.

Back in the suite, the air conditioner didn't work. The room was muggy. Opening windows in a jungle was not an option and it would just invite the hot air inside. The suite was dimly lit. I was busy looking for scorpion babies and mamas as I packed my bags. Ted called the front desk and ask that we be transferred to another villa.

Two bellmen showed up from the front office just a building away, with a golf cart. They helped us pack and moved us, and our belongings, closer to the entrance of the resort. We bumped along on the cobblestone driveway in the dark. The Honeymoon Suite, Cottage #29, had a small bridge over a ten-foot wide pool moat around two sides of the patio, which was enclosed with a cobble stone wall that matched the road with a locked door.

Everything seemed to have made the transfer except my watch. We called the bellmen and they had not seen it.

"I thought there was low crime here?" I whined.

"Low crime, not no crime. You made that too tempting for them. At least you have your jewelry, and besides, it might show up tomorrow," Ted comforted.

"It was an Omega watch from my father before he passed. The beginning, the Alpha when I got the watch, was exactly 25-years ago. I loved that watch as much as one could love a material possession. It's been all over the world with me. I feel his presence and protection through that timepiece. I'm heartbroken at the thought of losing it," I recalled.

"It's after 11, let's call it a day," Ted pleaded.

I looked at Ted's watch and it was 11:11 p.m.

# CHAPTER 19
# COSTA RICA SAILFISH

In the morning, we walked to the dining area for a quick breakfast and to look for the two-tone Omega watch on the path. We didn't find it.

A small plane flew across the jungle expanse as we waited for our omelets at the restaurant.

"Remember when we flew in that small death-trap rusted plane to the beach area in the Dominican Republic? The wind kicked it around so much. I thought for sure we were going to crash in that jungle. You would never be found in that dense plant covering. You would surely be devoured by the insects and animals within the first hour. Scary stuff! Flying over the Everglades to Key West wasn't much more fun in the same size plane. He flew so close to the ground that we could see the alligators' eyes. The tin-can flight from Key West to Cuba still makes me shudder, too," I said.

"But then we had some better experiences on small charter and private planes. On Seabourne from San Juan to Beef Island in the BVI was exhilarating. I love Tortola. The flight from Miami to Saint Barths was exciting dropping into the short runway on the beach over the mountain. The seaplane from Key West to Ft. Jefferson was a fun snorkel adventure," bragged Ted.

"Then .... Captain Ed dropped us off on Cat Island! Oh, my! They gave no tickets, just everyone sitting around with no air conditioning. Then we finally took off several hours late on a pot-holed runway. They threw the luggage through the opening in the wall onto the broken conveyor belt. We still have a credit with Pineapple Air for the four hour delay. I don't think I'll use my free ticket," I laughed.

On the morning 20 minute drive from Villa Caletas to Los Suenos marina village, we passed brown-skinned women with straight hair pulled into buns. They wore white t-shirts, shorts and sandals. They were escorting children in Catholic school uniforms in small packs.

"Do you think this culture is easier to rule, without much policing or military, because the people are homogeneous? Look at them. They all look virtually the same and it appears they share a single religion with all those plaid uniforms," I asked.

"Sure, it's like when the United States was founded, everyone was in agreement of who we were and what our values were. Now the melting pot is chaotic and we should not be surprised at our internal feuds," he responded.

As we pulled into the marina, a Marriott looked surreal in contrast to the native living conditions. The resort marina had manicured landscaping like the gated communities of Palm Beach Gardens.

The marina was bustling with energetic anglers racing around on the floating docks. We boarded a 42 foot custom fishing boat Ted had chartered before.

The captain and mate gave us a quick hello and dutifully got the lines and told us, "We're going to Craters today. We should get your sailfish!"

The captain pointed to an ominous edifice looming in the foggy bay on the left, "That's the new Croc's Casino in Jaco beach."

He rambled as he and the mate set up nine light tackle rods, "In the charter business here in Los Suenos, we fish 200 times a year. Not much tide because so close to the equator, so generally we predict smooth boating conditions. In the Caribbean islands, you can be stuck on land for days waiting for a rage to pass. I love to fish but it's a burn out. I'll never see that casino because I'm too tired at night."

"It's sailfish season December to March, then marlin season till April or May. February and March are always the best," said the captain.

"I'm always here in March because that is the windy month in the Bahamas," said Ted.

"It's consistently hot and full-on fishing season here year-round. I had a record 32 marlin bite since you were last here. Ridiculous! Anglers waste their time in the Virgin Islands or Bahamas. There are no slips available and you have to buy a $1 million or more condo or house in Los Suenos to have the privilege then to buy a $100,000 slip. The guys pay because the fish bite here," persuaded the captain.

He offered us bottled water and continued, "Sure you can get to the Bahamas from Palm Beach in half a day. It takes 62 hours to motor a boat to Los Suenos. But watch, we'll be fishing, more importantly catching, in five, and we can fish every day."

He slowed the engines and put out a daisy wheel and the lines.

"Two jumping dolphins, that is a good omen," I pointed to Ted.

The mate gave me fishing instructions of how to hook sailfish, "Hook him. Release the drag. Pull the lever to the bottom. Let the fish run 3 seconds or so. Point the rod at the fish. Then lift the rod and tighten the drag by pulling up the lever. Then reel as fast as possible."

Captain Ed in the Bahamas generally set the gear so I had less steps to do. I practiced moving the lever a few times.

"We use circle hooks for billfish so we can let the fish go easily without much harm to the fish. The down side is, they jump and try to throw the hook out of their mouths," said the mate.

The captain had fished with Ted before and knew he was a seasoned angler. The mate met us for the first time. Both crew members were short. I was taller than both of them. They looked much larger on the website. I constructed travel websites. Everything looks enhanced on a website. Us marketing people make people bigger than life, sometimes literally.

We trolled in 83 foot depth at 8 knots at the underwater ledge.

"Birds and bait fish, we're about to have a show," Ted pointed out signs of fish to the crew.

Ted had a keen eye on the water and an intuitive sense for fish.

"Bam," the first line screamed as a huge sailfish jumped into the sky.

"This is the sailfish you've been waiting for Charlotte," cheered Ted.

I forgot about the whole drag business, and just started reeling like crazy. The mate wanted to give me instructions but just stared at me and watched me pull the sailfish up to the leader line in ten minutes. I reeled in slower so the mate could then hand line in the last ten yards and carefully pull the giant pelagic next to the boat to release the sailfish back to the water.

"A 70 pounder in ten minutes! This is your first fish?" asked the mate.

"My first sailfish. I've caught marlins larger than 70 pounds. My first was 350. Ted's taken me out in the Bahamas and Palm Beach a bunch of times targeting sailfish but I never seem to catch one. It's my last pelagic to catch," I said, adrenaline rushing through my body.

"Here in Costa Rica, a 100 pounder is a large sailfish, with typical range being 40 to 80. Sailfish are much smaller in Palm Beach and you don't have to put out kites and balloons here either," noted the mate.

Another line screamed and the mate yelled, "We're gonna' raise some fish today. It's gonna' be a blood bath!"

Ted and I took turns reeling in a dozen of the large sailfish, one after another. I practiced manipulating the drag. I had my sailfish, my goal, so now I could try new techniques to do even better. I was a competitor no matter what the sport. I had been reincarnated many times and I always said I was half male.

The captain said he moved from the States to Costa Rica for the fishing and stayed for the culture and lifestyle.

"Costa Rica, and especially Los Suenos is different than the Bahamas. The docks are only used by Gringo condo owners, so there is pride. The local Ticos work there, so there is pride again that they have this stellar marina in their country where they have lived for generations," said the captain, "Versus the Bahamas where blacks are running the marinas, after forcibly being brought there as slaves a few generations ago. It's a different attitude and work ethic of free men. The marina is run and managed totally differently."

We docked in time for happy hour at The Hook Up restaurant at the marina.

"This menu is right out of the Southern U.S. Listen to this, 'barbeque pulled pork with mango slaw and jalapeno cornbread,'" I noted.

"These anglers are all the same guys in the Bahamas. The Bahamas and Southern U.S. were both founded by similar European settlers, at the same time, so sure, it's all the same Southern culture. Then these guys brought The South here to Central America. The bread here is sweet like Bahamian bread, too," said Ted.

"You are sweet. Thank you so much for taking me on this sailfish adventure. It's a goal achieved after many years! Now I have to come up with goals for new adventures," I winked.

## CHAPTER 20
## CREEPY CRITTERS

We drove back to Villa Caletas and took quick showers after fishing. Ted played tango-beat music on his iPad.

"Care to dance senorita?" he flirted as he held out his hand.

We whirled around the villa for two songs.

"The private dance lessons in Buenos Aires come back after a few steps but I don't think I'll ever be on stage with my dance moves. My mother was a dance and theatre major in college. I didn't get the dance gene ... or the singing gene," I said.

"Being on stage doesn't mean you got a singing gene. Remember Cinderella at the Paris Opera House? We left at intermission and gave away our tickets to a pair of very ecstatic gay men," Ted said.

"We left because you were disappointed that Cinderella was rotund, not because of her lack for singing talent," I corrected.

"Pow. Pow," Ted said and pretended to shoot chatty chirping birds in the trees outside.

"You are a pretty good shot yourself. Remember bird hunting at the private estancia in Argentina? And the clay shooting in the Dominican at Casa de Campo?" asked Ted.

"We've played all over the planet. I admit, I really can't remember it all until you mention it," I said.

"We have fun together. You are my favorite person to give a gift. You are like a little kid. You get so excited. In our last trip to the City, we saw a pink bag in a window on Madison walking back to the Plaza after dinner at Daniel. We walked back the next morning to Chanel to buy it. It was named Trendy CC. Perfect for you! Then you spent the next two days photographing everything in New York City with your new pink prop. The creativity never ends with you. I never get bored," he said.

"And the best part is, you only took 15 minutes to make the purchase. You didn't want to see all the other options the sales guy laid out," Ted said.

"I'm a buyer not a shopper. I know what I want intuitively and immediately. I like nice things but I'm not hung up on collecting material things," I said.

"You don't need material things to make you happy. You are the happiest person I know," said Ted.

"I live in the moment. In the moment I choose to be happy. It's pretty simple," I said.

"Speaking of Trendy CC and happy moments, remember when you were the American movie star Cece? I told the people in the small old-school tango bar in Buenos Aires that you were a movie star. I bought a round of drinks for them all and they wanted your autograph? Fun times," said Ted.

Ted called the front desk clerk as the driver was late. She told us he was waiting for us outside of our villa. A $20 taxi each way on the winding hilly, cliffy ride in the dark, was a bargain we agreed.

We walked out as he pointed and exclaimed, "Look, a tarantula!"

A plump tarantula was sunning on the 12 inch round grey stones of the wall, with his furry eight legs spread out to nearly eight inches, right beside the door knob. No wonder the driver didn't knock!

On the way to Bambu at the marina village, the expressive taxi driver explained that many people have tarantulas as pets. The spiders are not typically aggressive he assured us.

He pointed out a coral snake crossing the road a few feet from our walled villa, "There are two types of coral snakes here, one is not poisonous. There are a lot of poisonous things here. Even with crocs and scorpions and tarantulas, we still have more people die each year in car accidents."

He spoke in perfect English, and I asked, "You are from Costa Rica?"

"Yes, I study English with Rosetta Stone. English is important to our business. We start learning English in second grade. I want to improve myself, so I want to do business with Americans," he said.

Over dinner Ted recapped fishing, "So you caught your sailfish! In Palm Beach they would have been 15 to 30 pounders. Here you caught 50 to 70 pounders and a boatload of them! And did you notice the partner fish? Her larger mate was on my line. He was dancing above the water line trying to shake the hook loose. The smaller partner joined the hooked sailfish twirling in mid-air beside him like a water ballet. We saw a magnificent show of nature that few people will ever witness."

Ted had a tear in the corner of his eye. He was as tender as he was tough at times.

I held his hand and said, "You cannot tame that which is wild, but you dance with it. I would dance for you."

The perfectly speaking taxi driver was waiting for us when we asked our server to call us a taxi, "He is in the parking lot."

The middle-aged driver engaged us, looking in the rear view mirror, uncomfortably so for me, while driving on the narrow dark roads leading up to Villa Caletas.

When we got to our villa, we all searched for the spider. We didn't see him. The driver pointed out a dark image hiding in the grout of the privacy wall only a few inches from where we saw him last. His eight furry fat legs were piled up one upon another so he would fit between the stones.

"Look, he's scared also. Poor little guy! He's hiding from predators himself. That must be how he lived to grow so big and fat, from hiding so well!" I said.

The men got the door open and Ted ran in over the bridge and opened the lock to the villa, then motioned for me. We had to dodge a pair of the Chihuahua size grasshoppers. Ted and I locked the door behind us and shook our heads laughing. The doorbell rang to the outside door. Ted reluctantly went outside to talk to the driver.

"Do you want me to kill him?" the driver asked.

"No. He didn't hurt us. He belongs here," Ted answered, and locked all the doors behind him.

Ted then ignored me and spent an hour researching tarantulas on his iPhone. His zest for intellectual knowledge intrigued me. Sometimes it annoyed me, when he ignored me. I spent the hour searching the linens of the bedding and the entire room for anything creepy or crawly as he read off to me facts of tarantulas.

"The driver spoke so fondly of tarantulas. Do you think the one at our door that didn't move, waited for his owner to return because he was a pet?" I asked Ted.

"Quite possibly. I thought the same thing. It was part of his shtick. I'm glad I told the driver not to kill the critter. We are isolated out here at the entrance in this private honeymoon suite," he pointed out.

The picture window of the jungle in the bathroom did not have a window covering. The light had attracted a swarm of the giant grasshoppers clinching to the glass.

"We are not alone," I affirmed, wondering what else was watching from below. I gave both the iPhone and the flip phone quick checks before climbing into bed.

# CHAPTER 21
## LAWS OF THE JUNGLE

We had a quick breakfast next to the iguana.

"You know, the tarantula thought, 'They can't see me!'" I poked at Ted.

"Ha! So many times we think people can't see us! It started our first trip to Nassau. The waiters at the French restaurant holding the silver trays with their white gloves singing love songs in unison as they served. We docked Blue Daze right there at Atlantis by the restaurants. Apparently, I thought people couldn't see in the boat while we were changing clothes. Then came screaming in Captain Ed to tell us otherwise!" chuckled Ted.

We drove ten minutes to Carrera National Park to meet a guide named Enrice for a private eco tour arranged by the hotel. The 40-something in tan, olive and camo, had a wide genuine smile. Except for his textured facial skin, he could have been an Armando candidate in Italy or Spain. But our guide grew up in one of the tool sheds and not in the villas on the Mediterranean Sea.

We met him in the parking lot of the park. He encouraged us to spray ample bug repellant as he coated himself.

He started the tour with, "In Costa Rica we have 139 snakes, 22 poisonous including sea snakes. We have 17 vipers that grow up to nine feet and lay eggs like birds."

"I didn't come here to see snakes. We've already been introduced up close to tarantulas and coral snakes. On this tour, I'd like a toucan and lots of monkeys please!" I requested.

"Toucans, ok, we have over 900 species of birds in Costa Rica and half of them are represented in the park," the guide agreeably changed subjects.

"Carrera is an indigenous name meaning 'River of Crocodiles' because we have the second largest population of crocodiles in Costa Rica living here. They are much larger and meaner than your Florida alligators. They live in the Tarcoles River, where 50 percent of our population also lives on the riverbanks. We have nearly 6 million citizens. We are a peaceful culture. We should sometimes be not so peaceful. We have concerns about people moving here. We are 76 percent Roman Catholic from Espana. The surrounding Venezuelans and Hondurans would like citizenship. You are on the Pacific side and the Atlantic is the Caribbean side. Columbus visited one of our islands. The indigenous people were decimated during the Spanish conquest, starting 600,000 and now about 68,000 survived today," he rambled.

He pointed out a three-toed sloth and showed us through his binoculars.

"For mammals, we have sloths, bats, porcupines, anteaters, coatimunti which are raccoons with a long nose. We also have macaws," and he pointed to one in a tree above us.

"The park was donated by a wealthy rancher. The government one time divided his large farm and gave small parcels of land to the people. They couldn't afford seeds or equipment to farm the land so now there is one wealthy owner again. He donated the forest for conservation," he spoke in the same perfect English as the driver.

He pointed out plants along the narrow dirt path along the thick vegetation. He noted over 90 varieties of ficus plants live in the park. I remembered my yard man telling me one time that all the plants I babied in my yard started in a jungle in peril of a guy with a machete trying to clear a path. He must have visited Costa Rica. Enrice pointed out a Pelican's flower on a vine that attracts flies to pollenate.

"Are you sure you don't want to see a snake Charlotte?" he asked.

"No! No snakes," I answered definitively.

He paused and smiled and chose a fork to the left in the path. He pulled out a smart phone with a Costa Rica Bird Field Guide and looked up data to show us.

He set up a tri-pod with a spotting scope and had us take turns looking at a colorful Gantered Trogon and a hummingbird. An uptight gay male couple carrying extensive recording equipment snarled at us for talking. A small group of serious bird watchers appeared around the next corner of the path, none of who seemed to be having fun by my measure. It's like in golf tournaments when you can't talk on the sidelines, so why go?

"We have 14,000 species of butterflies, of which, 2,000 you would know in the U.S.," he said as he led us away from the group.

He whistled and snapped his fingers and another guide appeared from the dense foliage and led us to a new path.

"We have three monkeys in the park, holler monkey, white-faced monkey and spider monkey. They act like clowns. They eat fruit, leaves and flowers. These white-faced monkeys live in groups of five or six and communities of about twenty. They live for 40 years," the guide said.

"Now these guys are having fun!" I said and pulled out my camera to capture the sweet faces.

When I zoomed in, I could see the insects on their faces. Even the cutest of the cute wasn't comfortable in the jungle, I thought.

"So, sailfish and monkey checked off list, now for the toucan," I was ready to get out of the jungle as the insects were swarming if you sat still for one moment.

"The toucans you will see at your hotel after a rain. They move around after the rains," he advised, "But I'll show you macaws before you leave."

He took us to another section of the park and indeed the trees were alive with bright red, loud macaws mating.

"It's honeymoon time for macaws. They are mating and nesting and celebrating. They mate for life and live to be 70 to 90, longer than many people," the guide said and set up his tripod so we could see the bird orgy.

We walked back to the parking lot and Enrice asked, "Remember when I asked you if you wanted to see snakes?"

"I said no," I reminded him.

"Well, yes, you said you didn't want to see them, so I didn't point them out. Snakes slinked by you all day. You didn't see them. They didn't harm you. You can be around poisonous dangerous animals and not be harmed if you don't bother them," he smiled, "It's a law of the jungle."

# CHAPTER 22
## WILD RIDE IN TAXI 16

"Let's be honey sloths for a while, then let's be macaws," playfully suggested Ted flapping his arms like a bird.

Back at Villa Caletas honeymoon suite, we poured glasses of Tabali Chilean white wine. Through the picture windows, we watched the afternoon torrential rains bathed the forest in a cleansing coolness. I wondered where the tarantula might be hiding if he was wild and not the pet of the taxi driver. I looked in between all the sheets before we crawled in to cuddle.

"So, the snakes won't give me nightmares because I didn't see them. It's funny how fear works. You can be in great peril and if you don't know it, stay calm. Now, when we docked at the marina in Cape Eleuthera in the Bahamas, oh, I was afraid then. Massive sharks filled that marina. One little slip, and you would be engulfed in seconds. I remember watching Captain Ed clean the fish at that marina and the feeding frenzy as he tossed the heads and fish bones," I said.

"You were more afraid of the Bahamians at Rosie's Marina at Grant Cay. The one night we stayed there it was a waking nightmare for you. I've never seen you cling to me like that," said Ted.

"Well, they were so poor and remote from the world. It's inconceivable to think that island is in the Bahamas so close to civilization. The one woman kept following me around and begging for magazines. She was desperate for knowledge of the outside world," I said.

"And in another remote place, in the Dominican Republic, I was terrified driving through those sugar cane fields on those dirt roads. Remember we kept calling and leaving messages for Ed so somebody would know our whereabouts? The taxi driver picked us up at the airport and we were staying in that all-inclusive resort in Punta Cana. To get there, he had to drive us through remote farmland. He didn't speak a word of English and kept stopping at gas stations to ask for directions and men would hop in the taxi to help him find the resort. They didn't speak English either," I recalled.

"Channel 26! It was worth the travel of terror! In that one all-inclusive couples' resort, the TV station was set on a porn station. At the swim up bar, after a few drinks, everyone started comparing notes and chanting 'Channel 26!'" Ted laughed.

"Speaking of the Bahamas, when we saw the macaws and parrots today, did you think of Goldie?" asked Ted.

"Yes! That crazy caged bird in Harbour Island at the tiki bar at Ramora Bay marina! After seeing his family members, I see why he was so sex deprived living in the Bahamas. The macaws here are all sex maniacs," I acknowledged.

Ted mimicked the bird voice of Goldie and the birds' up and down seduction dance, "Fuuuccck?"

"Then I would shockingly ask Goldie, 'What?' and then he would pull back and mimic me and shockingly ask, 'What?' When we would walk away, he'd start the F-word again to lure us back to his game. He would flirt with girls and hang from his perch and try to look up their dresses and swimsuit wraps," I reminisced laughing.

"Goldie was taught his colorful language by the bartender," Ted laughed.

"That was ridiculous! After seeing that flirting frenzy today, I really feel sorry for Goldie. He was meant to mate for life, a very long life of maybe near 100 years. He was not meant to live in a cage. No human attention could give him what he desired, true everlasting love," I spoke for my feathered friend.

"Toucans!" I announced.

We ran outside with camera in hand, but no keys for the self-locking door and little clothes. We were nearly naked. The precautionary shoe-in-the-door maneuver failed with the excitement of the toucans. I got my shots of the Fruit Loops birds, and, thankfully, Ted got the door right before it clicked locked leaving us on the balcony over the jungle cliff.

Ted snapped photos of me posing in front of the lush greenery and said, "Remember when you were posing seductively like this in front of the big golden Buddha at Buddha Bar Paris in the upstairs bar?"

"Ha! Yes! Ann texted me telling me I should internet date. You said I should send her photos of the date that I was on with you. Hello, Paris! We have so much fun together," I said.

"Yeah, and those guys from East Germany really thought I had it good. I was drinking with this hot chick taking her photo, then you pulled out the cash I had given you to pay the bill. They really thought I was the coolest then. They were asking me how I got a hottie and one that pays," he laughed and puffed out his chest.

"You 'da man! You know, I don't always tell Ann or other friends about our adventures. If she's between boyfriends, I don't want to make her, or anyone, ever feel left out or not as fortunate. I never try to incite jealousy," I said.

"If she was in Paris she would post photos on social media nonstop. She would claim her date to be fabulous. She would brag," he said.

"I don't need validation from other people to know when I am happy," I said, adding, "I am blissfully happy in this moment. A moment is all we ever have anyway. I am present and grateful."

We decided to watch sunset from the moat pool surrounding the entryway in the courtyard.

"We are not alone!" I screamed and pointed under the small bridge to our front door with a swarm of tarantulas. We jumped out of the wrap-around pool and watched the gold sky turn to red and to lavender inside the honeymoon suite.

"Where is my belt?" Ted asked as we were getting dressed for dinner.

I closed my eyes for a few seconds, and said, "Look by the tub."

"You are so good at intuitively finding things," he laughed walking and holding the alligator belt.

"Remember when you lost your fluffy angora red scarf in New York City?" he asked, then answered, "And we walked around Midtown and had lunch then came back and it was in a snow drift on Park Avenue a block from the Waldorf right where it had fallen. Not a speck of dirt on it. Just waiting for your return."

"But ... you could not find our clothes after our skinny dip in Bimini! Remember the truckload of Bahamians pulled up on the remote coastal sand road and laughed at us for a few minutes. Then they took off. Luckily, they traded my new Crocks and left an old pair of tennis shoes. It could have been much more interesting if they had taken all of our clothes," he teased.

"We'd have to whack them. But you just can't go around whacking people anymore! Remember in the Fort Lauderdale Ritz bar by the pool? The debt collector man with his big scarred face and crooked smile was complaining about technology and how cameras and surveillance were hurting his career," I laughed.

"I do remember! What I don't remember at all is the New York trip when your meeting got cancelled," I said with a smirk.

He finished my thought, "We started with wine at lunch at Le Bernardin. The maître d thought we were so charming he brought us lemon drop shots. We then didn't recall our dinner or even if we had dinner! Wasted shot traveling in New York with all the trendy restaurants if you don't remember the dining experience!"

"Te amo," I seductively purred in a Spanish accent.

"Ha! When we were at that restaurant in Colonia Sacremento in

Uruguay practicing our Spanish. The couple next to us had to tell us we were saying, 'I love myself,'" responded Ted.

We decided to call anonymously from our cell phones for a driver to dinner. We didn't want the guy with the pet tarantula again. We had a pleasant cocktail hour at The Hook Up with the other anglers. Bragging and boasting abounded of massive mahi catches and coolers of tuna.

We indulged in Italian cuisine at Lanernia in the private upstairs dining room. It was our last night and we stayed late for extra wine. We started early in the room and stayed late at the restaurant and had a nice wine buzz.

We walked downstairs and asked the marina dock master to call a taxi. He said he would call taxi number 60 for us. We later realized this must be a code. We didn't want the tarantula driver. We got worse, the unseen snake.

"Do you see that guy, he's following us!" I pointed out a shadowy figure creeping and trying unsuccessfully to hide in the landscaping much like the tarantula trying to hide in the grout.

Ted instinctively gained composure, grabbed my hand and instructed me to walk quickly. He guided me to the taxi stand where the night prior a dozen taxis stood in wait.

"We are late tonight so no taxis are there," I pointed out nervously.

"The dock master called, so a taxi will be here soon. Don't worry," Ted assured looking around in the dark parking lot.

"There he is again!" I screamed pointing at the lanky hunched man hiding behind a median of tropical plants near us. I wanted him to hear so he would know he was not hidden.

The taxi pulled up after a nervous wait time. I jumped into the back seat, with Ted right behind me. The front passenger door flew open and the shadowy figure jumped into the front seat and told the driver, "I'm here for taxi number 16."

"This is 60! This isn't your taxi! Get out now! Driver, drive, drive, drive! Don't let this man in the car. Get us out of here now!" I screamed.

The car stood still. Both Ted's back door and the man's front door were still open. Lights turned on in the condo windows above the scene. The man's head jerked as he looked at the driver's face then ours. He froze for a moment, then got out slamming the door and disappeared back into the darkness.

"That was him! That was him! The Fugitive! The Fugitive from Port

Lucaya! He showed up in Palm Beach! What's he doing in Costa Rica?" I was alarming Ted.

"Villa Caletas please," Ted instructed the driver over my screams and tried to calm me.

The driver didn't speak, just stared at us wide-eyed in the rearview mirror.

"What fugitive? What are you talking about?" Ted asked screaming over my hysteria and holding me trying to calm me.

"I'll tell you in the villa," I said and waited for a very, very long 20 minute ride to pass.

We weren't sure if the tarantula was guarding the door but he felt like a minor threat. We bolted in and locked both outside and villa door.

"Do you think 60 and 16 were codes at the marina for robbing us?" I asked.

"There have been increased robberies of tourists and we might have seemed vulnerable. They didn't take into account your sixth sense," he speculated.

"Now ... The Fugitive?" he asked.

I reminded Ted of telling him about The Fugitive in Port Lucaya. Ted, of course, was with Captain Ed in Aspen in New Year's Eve 2013. Then I told him about two years later, this week, The Fugitive trying to convey messages to me.

"Not again. Not again," he said and left for the grasshopper clad window in the bathroom.

He undressed and stood in his boxers with his hands on his hips silent, staring out into the jungle with his lips pursed.

"Let's end this for once and for all," he said.

I wasn't sure if he was talking about ending me and my cyber baggage or ending the bad guys. I didn't ask. Potential relationship mishaps always seemed more manageable in the morning. Like the calm eye of a hurricane, our relationship was calm in an unhealthy way. While the high winds of controversy can stir waters of authentic resolutions, we stayed united instead on negativity avoidance, romance, adrenaline and humor. We created a perfect storm. It was much like my marriage, where the weather report looked sunny and mild on the outside. It was my Southern upbringing to be sweet.

# CHAPTER 23
# KEYS TO SUCCESS

We did what we had learned to do well, avoid conversation that would result in conflict. Both of us turned heads like owls continually in the transport, the airport, the airplane and the Miami airport.

In the baggage claim area, Ted asked, "So did you bring my leash?"

"Yes, of course," I responded

Overhearing our conversation, the elderly lady next to us, twirled around and stared in horror at what probably looked like a normal conservative couple. She backed up shuffle style to the opposite side of the room.

Through my hysterical belly laughing, I replied, "That is so funny. No telling what she thinks. Yes, I brought the surfboard leash so we can stay connected while snorkeling!"

Humor helped us heal our relationship rough spots so far. Thankfully both of us have a buoyant sense of humor. We hopped in my car and started heading south. The goal was Mile Marker One, the southernmost point in the U.S. in Key West.

"So, you still up for this trip or do you need to get back to Palm Beach?" he asked as he started my ignition and put the convertible top down.

"I want to stay as far away as possible for now. Let' drive south!" I said.

"This is just another reason I love you. Composure in the face of potential fear or threats," he smiled and motored out of the Miami airport.

"Why us? When I first met you, I found you attractive, but I didn't hit on you. I became enchanted quickly as I got to know you in a few short encounters. You had so many layers. It's hard to explain. You have a hot body and are sexy, but so conservative. I remember the third time I ran into you was in Winter Park. All the bullshit talk was going on around us. But we were talking and that's all I was aware of in the whole room. I was definitely listening," he smiled and reached over and grabbed my hand.

"You captivated me. Wham! I would normally just throw some bullshit lines out to a pretty girl. Not with you. Concepts came out that you lightly touched on. I wanted more. The temperature of the room grew warm, the lights were brighter, the whole space was a new environment. All I could think, was 'Wow!' You charmed me and we've lasted ten years. The meeting of soul mates! I didn't even know what that term meant. I was all business. I could flirt. You offered up the comfort food of conversation. I was hungry for real love; I had never tasted it," he said.

I turned my head to face him as he continued, "I wanted to talk more. You knew of spiritual things I had never known. Then in time, we added the combination of romance and that combination, all of a sudden, I was learning a whole new language of feelings, a spiritual connectedness. I had never experienced intense intimacy before. We became 'us,' one unit," he said.

"You've come a long way with your ability to describe love," I said, "I told you I had a reading in New York City in SoHo the week prior to getting to know you. She told me I would soon date three men and would marry one. I told you I was monogamous and had never dated three men simultaneously before. Three was a high sales goal! I asked if you would set me up with your friends. You said, 'I'll throw my hat in the ring,' then you never introduced me to anyone, except as your girlfriend! Remember?"

"Oh, I remember, I came to Winter Park and we had lunch at Dexter's. I was awestruck. I remember the table, the light, this nervousness. I didn't know what it was. I went fishing in Patagonia the next week. I was so empty and longing for you. You had clever conversation, not trite. Real, deep thought mixed with banter and humor. You emanated this vulnerability and innocence. I immediately responded. I wanted to protect the innocence in you," he flowed, and ended with a pregnant pause that I did not fill.

In my head, I thought, "I wish you had been with me more and protected me more."

He went on, "Before me was this beautiful, worldly, gentle soul who has so much faith in the concept of 'good.' I knew you were different. I later learned you were a spiritual messenger. It was overpowering to me as a businessman. You had access to this whole other world. You have this incredible perception and this presence of light. All I could think was, 'This girl has power.' I wanted to know more. Over time, I witnessed firsthand spiritual encounters with you. I would not say you are controlled by God, but certainly in sync with God. I am in awe of you still. You showed me praying, and healing, and how you lead a life of faith. Not by words but by example. I am never surprised. Nothing ever, ever surprises me when it comes to you," he said in the language of loving and caring that he had learned from me.

I had a lump in my throat. I felt like he had thought about our relationship in great detail. I had made the pros and cons list myself. I had the same feeling, like when you are packing your kids' rooms as they head off to college, and you find a stuffed baby koala bear on the closet shelf. The baby koala bear had a missing eye. Ted and I had a lot in our favor, but we had something missing, too.

# CHAPTER 24
## BOOK OF SAMUEL

"Remember when we bought God a Diet Coke in Book of Samuel?" I threw out one of our spiritual experiences that we had made humorous to change the course of the conversation. I was often amazed at how much detail Ted could recall about an incident. I would most definitely have to look at notes to bring such intense detail to light.

"We've been to the City about 20 times together, all memorable, but nothing beats the time you witnessed the spiritual world with me," I said.

"We saw 'Book of Mormon' on 49th, then went for drinks at the Peninsula on 5th Avenue and 55th Street. Around 6 p.m., we were the only people in the rooftop bar, Salon de Ning, at the Peninsula Hotel. God came in and perched on a bar stool next to you. He looked like a cast member of 'Book of Mormon.' He had a black and gray beard trimmed straight, chest length. He wore a top hat and long black coat. He wore a black formal outdated suit with the coat too long, a wrinkled strange white shirt buttoned to the top, and weird clunky black dress shoes. He seemed confused and was out of place. He seemed skittish and not at ease. He was looking around like he was lost. He was just sitting there by himself with nothing to drink. He didn't have on a watch or any worldly possessions. He was a large old guy with tallow skin. It was like he wasn't really alive. He touched you, so I know he was of flesh. Normally I would protect you from someone who looked strange, but it's Cat, so I said 'let's let this play out.' I've been with you on these spiritual adventures before," he said.

"I said hello to him. I introduced us and in a strange accent he responded 'Samuel,'" I said.

"He didn't speak English. He was staring at me studying my face. I asked him, 'Do you know me?' That felt more polite than to ask why he was staring. He reached for my right hand and turned it over to see my palm, which he studied for a few moments. He read my palm. Like palm readers, he seemed to grimace at the scars. The surfboard accident scar severed my life line. Hand readers have told me I'll almost die but live, two children, one marriage, another marriage later in life, a long life, medical issues due to stress and that I am a very old soul.

He studied the creases then leaned in and very excitedly started gesturing and speaking in a language we could not identify, maybe German or Russian, or something from the Middle-East, or an ancient language. He leaned in and was whispering very excitedly and loudly in my ear. I could feel the force of his breath blowing against my cheek. I remember he wouldn't let me take his photo," I recalled.

"Then I motioned to him with my hand like holding a pen. I said that you were a writer, I said 'scribe, scribe' and pointed at you. Then God took off his wire frame glasses and started crying," Ted said, "It was dramatic and poignant like right out of a movie scene."

"Samuel was holding my right hand and with his left hand pointing a finger and looking upward toward heaven then pointing to my heart and then his, all with tears down his face. He got down on one knee and bowed. He got back up and continued to hold my hand and continue with his excited words. I asked him, 'Do you know me?' He responded with more words I did not understand. Then I said, 'I will write your words. I promise.' Then in perfect English in his strange accent, he said, 'Thank you,'" I said shaking my head in awe still at the memory from several years ago.

"It was intense. Emotional. You cried. You never cry. There are a lot of writers in New York City at any given time. But he wasn't there to find them. It was so clear that he was there waiting for you. To tell you what he whispered in your ear. He communicated it even without speaking the same language," he continued.

"You went to the ladies' room and I paid for God's Diet Coke. I don't know why I ordered a Diet Coke. Maybe God would have liked a regular Coke or a Macallan like me. I was pretty sure he didn't have American currency. He kept sipping the bubbling brown sweetness and staring at the glass like he had just arrived through the time travel tunnel," he laughed.

"You know, that space would attract a time traveler as an attractive landing pad. When you look down from the view at the Peninsula rooftop bar, you see the spire and the round skylight below at Fifth Avenue Presbyterian Church. It was founded in the early 1800's after my mother's family was founding Presbyterian churches in Tennessee in 1794," I said.

"You tell the story that it was God, but he introduced himself as Samuel. You know who Samuel is, right? He was among the first prophets and anointed Saul and David as the first two Kings of Israel. He also came back in the flesh with Moses," I clarified.

"Then we had a late dinner at Le Grenuoille, and there Samuel was at the small six- person bar with his staring eyes again. I gave the Maitre D a $20 and told him to give God a Diet Coke. How did he beat us there? Then he appeared in phantom style at The Palace, the next place we went after dinner, three in a row. The Palace was strange so we didn't stay. It's not a place we would normally even go. In New York, you couldn't just appear in three totally different random venues if you tried. Your stalker could have trailed us with an iPhone, but how did God find us? Uncanny. Incredible. Unbelievable. If I wasn't with you, it would be hard to believe," he said.

"I wish I knew exactly what he said. I do get the gist through his hand gestures. I wish I knew exactly what I am supposed to do. I would do it. So many years waiting, then God sends Samuel right in front of me, and I don't understand what he's saying," I said.

In my insides I did know. I had always known.

"Let's stop for a Diet Coke, not a bad idea, ok?" was all I could muster as the intensity of the memory sank in to my consciousness.

We pulled over to a souvenir stand selling used lobster and crab crate buoys and handcrafted wood Tiki heads for garden art. I bought a metal sculpture of two lovebird parrots. My souvenir-memory from the Peninsula had more meaning and more impact on my life than any trinket from the northern Keys could have. I was again, like the snorkeling analogy, living at once in both the flesh and the spirit.

# CHAPTER 25
# THE AMERICAN DREAM

I got back in the car, and back inside my own head again. Ted was making business conference calls on his iPhone.

I actively sought answers during my divorce period 20 years ago, again after 9/11 in 2001. I have the same feeling again recently as I sense a new major paradigm shift brewing inside of me.

In 2001, after 9/11, the ad agency was sucking wind. I went through a significant spiritual growth period. I had two spiritual friends meet me on alternating Tuesdays for spiritual advice and mentoring. One was Margaret, who showed up years before to help me during the divorce. We went our separate ways and she showed up again after 9/11 at the same time as Donna. We met weekly at my kitchen counter and called our hour-long mentoring sessions happy hours. Margaret said she felt led by Spirit to give me confidence in my own psychic abilities. She helped navigate the stalker-filled year of Unlucky 13. She showed up again recently on yet another major shift.

The other mentor, Donna, I met at an ad agency pitch. She was a high-level executive with a start-up technology cyber safety company's board. In my first meeting with the group, she spilled that she was writing a book on God. She pulled me aside after my first meeting and quizzed, "So, I'd never tell these men about my spiritual work. Why did I tell you in front of them? Who are you?" We became fast friends. She became a spiritual mentor to me for a year. Neither of the women knew each other. I intentionally didn't introduce them. One week, one would tell me something about my life's path and purpose. The next week, the second, unknowingly, would validate the message. My own sixth sense accelerated as the teachers validated and gave me a vocabulary for spirituality I had experienced my whole life. I flipped my notebook and found a reading from Donna that I had started reading New Year's Eve.

DONNA, AMERICAN DREAM, Dec. 3, 2002 my notes read:

During the session Donna opened her eyes and laughing said, "Who are your family members? There is a whole room full of men here in funky black suits, weird shoes, and white wigs!"

"Could be a mayor from London, Isaac Pennington on my mother's side. Could be family members from Great Britain, Scotland, or early

America," I guessed, and pulled the sweater tighter as a chilling coolness permeated my body.

She went back into a quiet voice, "Your father wants you to bring back patriotism. His family had to make sacrifices and give up worldly things. He had a blind eye?"

"Yes, a fishing accident. He was an avid outdoorsman, hunter and fisherman," I affirmed.

"I feel them. They are 'Those People,' the American Forefathers who created America from God. Your ancestors played key roles. They put 'In God We Trust' on dollars. They believed in freedom for everyone and that every person is equal. America was different because they brought God to America. People are now trying to take God out. What you now call me, and people like me, 'New Agers' actually believe in exactly what your family believed. It's not new at all. This film you want to produce, 'Raising the Bar,' could be about finding love, but it's about what has happened to America. This is the film you will produce."

I interrupted her, "I don't know what has happened to America. I barely watch news. I don't follow politics. I'm not sure what I am being asked to do."

"You will. You will see," she said.

Donna continued with closed eyes, "The Constitution and the Declaration of Independence, your family was involved?"

"Yes, I don't remember all the names or details. I read every family chart and handwritten letter when I was choosing baby names. I remember on my mother's side, the name Reverend Alexander Craighead. He was one of the first settled Presbyterian ministers in North Carolina. He inspired through his preaching on liberty, the Mecklenburg Declaration in 1775, which was a precursor to the Declaration of Independence. Another on my mother's side, Reverend Samuel Doak, founded the first Presbyterian churches and the first college in what would become the state of Tennessee in 1794. Tusculum College is still co-ed, educating females way ahead of it's time, and still affiliated with the Presbyterian Church. There were some of the first City Council Members of Charlotte and a Governor of North Carolina. There were others. I have the names in handwritten letters my first cousin wrote to my mother in the 1970s when she was researching the family genealogy. Our mothers were the beautiful Carter girls, five of them, and one brother who took over my grandfather's law practice. My first cousin Rose Clayton married a man that was elected to the U.S. senate as a Republican for more years than any other senator. Her father was influential with Democrats. Our grandfather was mayor of his little Tennessee town outside of Memphis and served in the state House of Representatives a few terms. My father was a County Court Clerk. That's all I can remember without the notes. On my father's side, my genealogist aunt traced that family back 600 years from the U.S. settlers starting in Maryland, to England to Sweden. I do have those notes somewhere, too. I have a whole chart on that side of the family going back to the first American settlers," I said.

"You have a lot of heavy hitters of humanity in your DNA. There is a pattern of leadership you are being asked to follow. You can later look up who they were. This might help you and give you insights. You have many generations here in the room today," she said.

"They are passionate and they are pissed, the whole room! You will know because you will see a rise in resistance to fundamental American beliefs. Evil twists will speak our truths differently. Your ancestors knew to honor God and it doesn't matter how you get to God. The fundamentalists and the New Agers believe the same in pursuit of happiness, freedom of religion, freedom of speech. They were successful prosperous people who gained prosperity through being philanthropists and spiritual workers. These guys did 'it.' Then Americans came here and we became what we left, like trying not to be your parents. Your ancestors are concerned that what they intended will be torn apart. There will be a big impact on politics. Government leadership has to be God-based and God-centered for America to continue as intended. The impact of wars will make people more able to listen as they look for answers. Make sure the intention is not destroyed. This is far reaching," she continued.

I was stunned and overwhelmed by her directive. She sat still for a moment shaking her head up and down in a nonverbal "yes."

"They have chosen you. Write about the resurgence of the American Dream," she said.

"I interview someone for a book or film? I'm personally not the ideal individual to represent my family or America," I balked.

"But you are. You don't have to be perfect. Imperfect makes you real to others. You sense and know the American Dream. You live it every day more than you think. You are a mix of many graces. The root of you is a light being and an earth mother. You have to stop being an 'It Girl.' You can't be cool and with the in-crowd. That vibration will bring you down from where you need to be to do this work. You will be willing to give up your flitting around and socializing when the time comes," she said, raising more questions than we could answer in our hour session.

"You will feel like it's 'us against the world.' Step out in faith. Seems like I'm talking crazy! These men are showing me what you are to do. There is a leading group among the first pilgrims, an elite group of four guys and their wives. It fell apart. Through generations, I see a womanizer, and an alcoholic. Lineage is missing now, not as direct. In your life, live up to heritage. Overcome the bar. Surpass. Believe in Spirit. Write as a memoir, as edgy opinionated art. Be prepared to get the information and be a part of the process. Get rid of shame and fear of bringing New Agers to light. Know that our founders had the same belief system. You will be hugely involved in a spiritual revolution. Like your ancestors, be a promoter of The Dream," she predicted.

# CHAPTER 26
# INDEPENDENCE

One week an astrologer friend filled in for Donna. She introduced me to several of her New Age friends all with different spiritual disciplines. They all told me similar predictions.

The astrologer notes from Nov. 7, 2002 read:

"Huge psychic capacity. Purpose is to find strength within self. Stand alone and develop leadership. Reliance upon oneself. Struggle alone but know that God is with you. Link your heart and creativity and be a leader for others to teach self-esteem and how to be creative. You have a martyr / savior pattern. You struggle with people deceiving you to use your strength to take care of them. You are vulnerable to your many past-life soulmates because of a strong desire for love in this life. Following a period of isolation, you will cultivate being creative to energize and enthuse others. Don't let people become dependent on you. Revolutionize tradition. Use your unique eccentric gifts to break the antiquated structure of family to now be fair and equitable. Show how others can be independent. You have a big vision to show freedom and originality as a shining star. You will be an inventor for large groups of people. Your desire is good for humanity. It's big in scope. You will be responsible for the structure of the group."

There was more but I stopped reading. I had the astrological chart with an interpretation but the document itself looked voluminous and the content was overwhelming. The same group of terms popped up whomever I was consulting: spiritual, leader, creativity, star, family, humanity, secret.

The isolation theme was a common element as well. As much as I had avoided that period of my life, it happened anyway without my control. During the cyber stalking periods in 2011 and 2013, a natural isolation occurred. When you are being cyber stalked and cyber bullied by an insane man, people pull away. Some pulled away because of their own safety. I actually encouraged this even with my own children. Others pulled away because they just didn't want to deal with negativity. They wanted me to be the party planner and party girl and perform whatever usefulness I had in their life. I was surprised and disappointed at some of the people who left my life during that time. When I got grounded again, I didn't bring them back to my inner circle. The friends, both old and new, from that period of my life are my forever friends. I am eternally grateful for their support under such horrific circumstances.

This particular page looked like maybe my Southern girl training for male – female love relationships needed a review. I was a leader in any other aspect of my life. In a love relationship, I was willing to take a second seat. I considered that I'd like to try the totally equal version of a love relationship. The Age of Aquarius was impending which would bring women and men in an equal power balance.

I put down my notebook and looked at my handsome boyfriend Ted. "I'll start practicing with him," I thought.

# CHAPTER 27
# NINE AND ELEVEN REASONS TO LOVE AMERICA

I flipped back in the notebook to journal notes from 9/11 in 2001. The words brought back the memory in vivid detail.

Sept. 17, 2001 an e-mail to friends saved in my journal read:

"Return from Rome ... 'I MAY BE IN ROME, BUT MY HEART IS AT HOME,' said the handwritten sign topping the mound of flowers on the lawn of the American Embassy in Rome. I stayed the last few days at the Westin Excelsior next door among foreign dignitaries, international secret service men, and lots of machine guns. We were on the floor of Middle Eastern leaders all connected with 10 inch cables going into all the rooms and each with a personal guard at the door.

I flew out to meet 52 people on the TV station client trip last Sunday from Orlando to Newark to Rome to Porto Cervo in Sardenia. Monday poolside at the Hotel Cervo, 3 p.m., 10 a.m. NYC time, we learned of the terrible terrorism tragedy involving in part an airport we had flown out of a day prior. The shock and the mourning were compounded with homesickness and concern for our safe return to our families. Since there were no flights out anyway, we somberly continued with our itinerary.

Mid-week we flew to Rome as planned. Friday at noon, Rome called for three minutes of silence in honor of the American loss. Noon found me at the exact center of the Pantheon learning of the open-air top and the drain below in the temple. Powerful moment. As people prayed for America in languages from across the globe, if you ever doubted there was a God, you felt His presence in this ancient place of worship at this time in history. My skin tingled for hours.

Yesterday Continental flew us to the U.S. No flight attendants or Diet Cokes, but pilots and security guys with guns. Fine. The gruesome sight of the smoking abyss in the NYC skyline as we departed the plane in Newark to Orlando International began our reality of returning home.

I'm tired. I'm home. I'm still moving tomorrow to the new house.

I love America. Be strong. Leave your investments in place as we open the exchange today. Love, Charlotte

''Tis better to have loved and lost than never to have loved at all.' – Alfred Lord Tennyson"

A year later, in Sept. 2, 2002, a personal journal entry read:

"As I reflect back upon my last year since 9/11, the things I have loved have been plentiful and the things I have lost few.

That week, my son saw me cry as I unpacked our new kitchen and he watched the 'Star Spangled Banner' song to open a Gator game on TV. He rushed over to hug me with "Mom, are you ok? I've never seen you cry."

I told him, "I am saddened because you will never experience in the same way the America I have loved."

I have loved my 9-year-old daughter and 11-year-old son. I have reached age 40 in its glory and maturity and wisdom and maintained some of (lots of) my youthfulness along the way; I have loved that I still enjoy life. Everyday. I have loved my friends and family and the experiences I have shared with them. I have loved that I appreciate the profound enlightenment I often experience in the daily exchanges. I have loved the abundance received by my advertising agency as my clients sought consulting to stay competitive in a challenging market. I have loved that my contribution in all of these relationships makes a difference in the world in some small way.

Have lost. What I have lost on a Friday a year ago, at the center of the Pantheon in Rome at noon during a three minute period of silence where tour groups from every continent prayed for America, was myself as I had known me. At that moment, I was not sure I would get home. I have lost my naive sense of protection and security. I have lost the notion that freedom comes without a cost or without work. I have lost the belief that Good overcomes Evil simply because Good exists. I have lost any desire to be one hair less than the character that would fulfill my purpose or to surround myself with anything or anyone that is contrary to my core beliefs or values.

I shared Life cereal this morning with my 9 and 11-year-olds. And the day began. My life. This afternoon we will list 911 things we are thankful for today. We will deliver the hand drawn cards thanking the Winter Park fire and police departments for protecting us. We will rejoice in God's protection over us this past year."

Sept. 11, 2011, A Decade After Doom, a personal journal entry read:

"The house I moved into the week after 9/11 is long unpacked, lived in, paid for, and recently redecorated as children went to college. As I packed my daughter's room, with stacks of sketches and drawings, I ran across the pencil sketches of Dalmatians in fireman hats with buildings with smoke and stick people falling in the skies. It captures a chilling memory for our children and our culture.

I watched on TV the news clips I didn't see ten years ago because I was overseas and saw only CNN. I've continued my life and have stamped over a dozen countries on my passport since 9/11. I'm not afraid to travel or fly. I'm more determined through experiencing that day to continue to have a productive stellar life, continue to learn about other cultures, and live in and contribute to a country that is a world leader in every way.

Besides the World Trade Center, the other edifice for me that defines 9/11 is the Pantheon because of the spiritual moment there. My directive as a professional communicator to create Good Works has been the focus of my last decade for my life's purpose.

For the last 30 days I've worn the cross necklace I bought at the Vatican two days after 9/11. It reminded me each morning to love God, love America, love my life, and all the people in it."

## CHAPTER 28
## FILMS AND FAMILY SECRET

I flipped to Memorial Day in May 2002. Ann and I traveled to Naples and found a spiritual store on 5th Avenue. I had a crush on a guy there but it was going nowhere since I had to raise children in Winter Park. I loved introducing my friends to readers, then having girl talk afterwards. It was easy to listen to a friend's reading and see if I thought the reader was accurate. When they read me, sometimes the message was the me of the future, and it seemed so improbable that I would actually be that person. Nonetheless, I continued my marketing research of my life and kept notes.

May 25, 2002, my journal from Naples read:

"Your perfect date… high standards. If he doesn't open the door for you, you think he has bad breeding. Old school. Treat you like a lady. Wine and dine and the man pays. List of hoops if man to be in your life. He has to perform. Relax your rules. You have a Vivian Lee, Blanche, Southern attitude. Character flaw to be judgmental and critical to yourself and others. What do you do? (advertising) I see writing. Script writing. Screen writing. You are a natural. Dry wit. Way with words. Glib. Aptitude. Like 'Postcards from the Edge.' Ten ideas at any one time. Write. Snowball. Independent films. Mind goes quickly. Wasted 20 years. Your stuff will stand out. Notoriety from film industry. Savannah important like the 'Garden of Good and Evil' and the Southern culture, Flannery O'Connor, 'The Prince of Tides,' French Quarter and New Orleans, Hidden family secret to bring to forefront. Layer upon layer uncover family secrets, unravel something that started 150 years ago, maybe more. So, 150 years ago is 1852."

Wow! If I wasted 20 years then, now it's 14 years later, that's 34 years of wasted years? I wish my parents were here so I could ask what the family secret is, if they even knew. They didn't talk much about our family history. When my fiancée and I were deciding which church to marry in, then I learned of the long line of Presbyterian ministers. My mother told me about a Mayor in London, Issac Pennington. I remember thinking that would be a cute name for a baby, Pennington, and if it was a girl call her Penni. She told me about all kinds of political and civic leadership positions held in the past by the family but I simply don't recall what she said after so many years.

On my dad's side, I learned that I was related to Tennyson when I came home in second grade and asked only because my teacher asked. They were humble and didn't offer information unless you asked. I wish I had asked more. That side was from a long line of ministers in England before they moved to America as well.

I remembered little from my childhood. My memories are like cake batter all mixed and gooey until I became independent and an adult and the cake baked into something tangible. When I met with friends, they would recall events in such great detail. I was always living in such deep concentration of the moment. It's how you are supposed to live anyway, in the moment.

I was feeling car sick from reading. I rummaged around for my jewelry bag. I pulled out the two-tone cross necklace from The Vatican from 9/11 week and fastened it around my neck. I sighed.

"Why so serious?" inquired Ted.

"America is a relatively young country. Do you think it will stand the test of time?" I asked.

"We've visited many ruins and relics of cultures that didn't last forever, but America is special. The people have certain core values that will endure," he said.

"But we only last as America while the core values are present," I speculated.

Changing the subject, he said, "We'll last forever. I love you. Only you."

He always said that. His words were charming. I was a word person so I liked these words. If only his words and actions were in sync.

# CHAPTER 29
# LIGHTS, CAMERA, CALLING MEL GIBSON

I got a text from my son regarding his upcoming birthday trip with me to the Bahamas. Wagon rides and tricycle marathons were now replaced with weeklong fishing trips. The years sped by so quickly.

I remembered his 13th birthday in 2004. I found a page from March 26, 2004. The car hummed along as I read to myself.

The journal notes were about me firing five of my clients in one week from the ad agency. I was journaling my concern for income and for my future. The notion to fire all the clients came from an intuitive message that I followed. The intuitive message was inspired by a church sermon.

POTTERY BARN CALL March 26, 2004 notes read:

"I think I'll stop working and call and order my son's 13th birthday gifts. He likes my Pottery Barn chair at my home-office desk so I'll order him a chair from Pottery Barn Teen to encourage more A's and practice for becoming a partner in his dad's law firm. The telephone marketing person who answers the 800-number introduces herself as Kim. She asks how I'm doing while she processes the order and I respond that I'm not having a good day. She begins with light conversation. As I validate her responses, she goes deeper. After a few minutes, I realize she's giving me a reading and I begin to take notes: You have so much love. I can feel your love. You have the seat of authority given by God. Don't let them intimidate you. (Unethical business clients.) You are ethically right. Congratulations for not compromising on what you believe. Principle matter. Refuse to bend. Test. You are passing. Greater reward. Thrown at you to see if you are ready. He has to trust you to promote you to greater in the marketplace. He has chosen you for this. It's been a long time but it is coming. He loves you. A lot of people tried to walk on you and talk about you but the labels don't stick because what they say about you isn't true. He's increasing you to a Fortune 500 level. This is small. Really small. How much greater there is to come. You are a worshipper. Because of your lifestyle. That is what worship is, how you live your life. You drip with favor. He favors you because of your mercy to others. You see the good and forgive, and that is what allows you to go on. You pick yourself up and don't stop. Your son is watching you and he will be great. He's learning leadership from you. You walk in so much love because you know God every day the way you live. Your life pleases Him because you honor Him. After your bad moments, you walk in God, so you don't stay down long. It's hard to be a leader. Called to set trends. Not easy but worth it. Your persecution as a spiritual leader will be rewarded. Your children see not to follow, no airs, just be yourself, you are real to them. You cry but you don't stay there. Full of tenacity. You are a blessing to others. Now time to give back to you multiplied what you gave to others. Watch what he does. Promote you highly. This time they can't stop it. You needed humbling to be a leader to listen to Him better. You're so cool. You were made to exceed greatness. You have a right to it because the way you honored God since you were a little girl. You'll be president or CEO level of a fortune 500 company. God will put it in trusted hands. In all areas of your life you are worthy to God because you refuse to be less than His standard. Be encouraged. I feel your love. That is why I started talking to you this way. Ask specifically and you will get it. It's your trust. You're not crazy. I had to tell you. I'm in awe of what I see about you. He's pouring on you from every direction. He'll send people to show you spirituality. Watch. It's going to overtake you like a tsunami wave. Great rewards. Creative writing. Desire to walk in obedience. Enemy will tempt. When you cry, you never cry alone. Four angels surround you. You're a small-framed taller person. You are an intercessor. You pray for others. He attends to your desires quickly because you are swift to obey him. You will be a Mel Gibson in years to come. (He just released the movie "The Passion." Ok. I'm listening now.) You are that level. You can multi-task. Doors opening. Not miss a beat as you walk through all the doors. You have been prepared for this. You've passed tests and being sent into a new realm. A realm is higher than a level. You will progress because you fought for what God taught you."

Back in the moment beside Ted in The Keys, Louis Armstrong was singing, "What a wonderful world..." I pulled out my Go Pro camera. The palms were passing so quickly like the years of my life. I hit the red record button to record B-roll of the scenes from the convertible to use in future films. I hoped not too much more in the future. Too very many palms had passed.

# CHAPTER 30
# KEYS CONVERSATIONS CONTINUE

Ted was glassy-eyed driving south on the two-lane A1A.

"Yes, room service, I'd like a French toast, an omelet with extra cheese and spinach, an eggs benedict, a side of bacon, a side of fruit, a bowl of whipped cream, a cappuccino, an orange juice, and hot tea," I mimicked him in a whisper.

"Ha! The Breakers room service and the $600 bowl of whipped cream, which is all I wanted," he chimed in.

"Ready for a relaxing bubble bath?" I asked coquettishly.

"Oh, noooo! Only showers! I haven't had a bath since Napa! Or was that in Sonoma? Remember at Auberge du Soleil when I took the sachet and emptied it into the bubble bath? Ha! I was supposed to put the sachet in the bath, not the contents. I'm a man for God's sake. How do I know particulars of seductive bathing procedures? Then we clogged the drain and I picked grape seeds and lavender stuck to hairs from all over my body for a week," he laughed.

"We had that big comfy tub overlooking the gardens, a nice champagne buzz, then when you grew your purple coat, we couldn't stop laughing." I added.

"I remember you read me your first manuscript for your first book. Also, in a bubble bath, in a claw foot tub overlooking the river in Santo Domingo, at Hostel Nicolas De Ovando on the Calle Las Damas. You were a vision of beauty with magical words in your soft voice floating from your lips like an angel," he said.

"Bubble baths and showers were a thing for us for a while. The intimacy of naked wet bodies after being separated, seemed a natural place for us to reconnect each time," I said.

"Also, in Santo Domingo on that trip to the Dominican, at that art gallery ..." he said.

I finished his sentence laughing as we often did, "and you got the award from the shop owner. And his mother brought out the special moonshine liquor from the back office and they all toasted your manhood! The shopkeeper told you if you bought me the amber heart necklace that I was looking at, and the big parrot love-bird oil painting, that you could get lucky. I overheard him and, without much thought, told him you had already been lucky some five times that day. I exaggerated a little but boy did he like that!" I said.

"Five times? Cinco? And the guy held up five fingers. Then he started hugging me, and slapping me on the back, jabbering in Spanish. He paraded me out to the men sitting on the curb drinking matte with their parked bicycles, and they all went off. The Spaniards have swagger, especially there mixed with black. Surprising to the Spaniards, white guys have a little swagger, too!" he joked.

"You two amigos cracked me up. The mother and I bagged the necklace and painting while you guys bragged about manhood. Men like being men. Men like being with men, anywhere in the world," I said.

"Men? What about the Dominican dogs?" he asked.

"I'd rather forget! Dominican dogs! The fornicating wild brown dogs all over Santo Domingo. Right before we shopped, the doggie couple copulated right in front of the restaurant. People just walked by on the busy pedestrian street. The cocoanut man continued cracking fruit with his machete. An occasional passer-by would try to scoot the amorous duo onto the sidewalk. Because we sat there an hour, we realized they were stuck together! They finally pulled apart with a very sore set of private parts! I'm blushing just thinking of it again," I said.

"On that same trip you gave me a Kama Sutra book. We opened to random page and decided to give it a try. Well, the four-poster bed was a tad high. It loosened my hip and I limped for a month. After a little minor surgery, I was ready to crack the book open again. I've always liked reading," reminisced Ted with a grin.

"Remember outside of Buenos Aires that the ranchers would maim a front foot of cats and dogs so they couldn't run away? If I were born a dog or cat, I'd certainly want to be born in the U.S. where we pamper our pets. As a human, I most definitely would choose America!" I added.

"Yeah, remember all the stray cats that kept trying to get on our boat in Venice?" he asked smiling.

"That wasn't me," I said quietly not smiling anymore. We drove in silence a few very long minutes, very long like when you are waiting for a doctor's diagnosis for a terminal condition.

Ted broke the silence, "You didn't get the bitch gene, did you?"

I said, "No."

I thought, "Yes. I just have this Southern-girl training that makes me be sweet on the outside and sour on the inside. I'm going to be sick."

# CHAPTER 31
## MERMAID AND MAD DOG

We flat-lined for a few minutes. We brought our relationship back to life with reminiscing about flats fishing. Ted seemed to choose his words more carefully.

"Let's go to Lor-elei for those key lime coladas!" I suggested.

"Yum and done," Ted agreed.

The gaudy mermaid sign signaled we were officially in The Keys. The water under the dockside open air bar was the color of a golden margarita and splashed up to the mangroves. A sea cow lumbered under the dock where we sat.

The singer, a dead ringer for Jimmy Buffet, crooned, "Son of a son of a sailor ..."

A pink Cadillac limousine converted to a small boat puttered by with a boatload of chubby 30-ish brunettes in matching two-piece bikinis singing to the live music. Beer belley-ed men blew smoke from Lucky Strike cigarettes that floated right to our table. Two college guys were doing shots and one was about to blow cookies.

"Only in The Keys, wellllll, not exactly, remember the crazy group of Southern fishermen at Hope Town who told us about jumping in the water to ride the giant sea turtle?" Ted laughed.

"We've been around a lot of characters," I agreed.

"Let's go to Ziggie and Mad Dog's for lunch instead of staying here. They can serve us quickly. I'm here to take care of my Cat," he suggested.

"Purrr-fect," I agreed.

Ted could read me like a book. Zany is his specialty. I can take it in smaller doses.

We pulled in to the Zagat rated historic restaurant that Al Capone and the Chicago mob started back in 1962. I ordered the yellowtail in citrus glaze.

My iPhone beeped. Ann texted, "Bad case of PFDS. Armando is cool and Armando Senior is adorable."

Ted glanced over and asked, "What's up with Antsy?"

"She's got Post-Fun-Date-Syndrome. That is girl talk for being giddy and in love and then 'poof' the fun ends. It's like our fun adventure this week, then you will run off to work. I'll have PFDS. I'm ok with my own PFDS because you always make things better when I see you again," I said.

"Do I say fun too much?" ironically, as I was asking Captain Fun, "My first boyfriend after my divorce said I talk about having fun too much."

"Because you do have fun! Why not? It's how we roll. That's why you found me," he smiled.

Another text came in from J, "Boat ok. Nothing new for The Project."

"Send her the Buddha Bar photos! Make her jealous!" he joked.

"It's J. He's reporting on Blue Daze. All A-OK," I said.

Another text from Ann, "Tix for Boar's Head Festival at Bethesda-by-the-Sea? Tix for Polo opening day? Tix for charity gala at Mar-a-Lago?"

I responded, "In Keys now. Will check dates."

"Ann must be staying, she's stocking up on event tickets," I reported to Ted.

"What happened to Mr. Wonderful of the week?" he inquired not really caring.

"One or both of them got distracted in Wonderland. The Palm Beach candy store has lots of sweet distractions. But you are my sweetness," I said.

Another Ann text clicked in, "Armando has shown me lively places in West Palm Beach, like Camelot rocks. Grato has amazing food. We need to go over the bridge more. We've been doing FaceTime with his dad. A's dad wants to meet me so he's bringing his boat from St. Barths here to PB. p.s. a SHOWboat!!"

I laughed out loud and told Ted, "Antsy is fishing."

# CHAPTER 32
# ISLAMORADA LOBSTER ROBBERS

We rushed over to the marina to meet our charter captain for a few afternoon hours of flats fishing. The snowy egrets begging for bait fish flew off the dock as we rushed to the skiff. We motored five minutes past the buoys and crab traps and got out to the clear four foot crystal clear water with the grassy bottom. Captain had the shrimp on the hooks. He turned off the motor and stood up in the back of the boat. He started poling around with a ten foot pole which he dug into the sandy shallow bottom to move the small vessel.

He reminded us in a quiet voice, "Now to bonefish is a calculated cast to an elusive fish. When you cast, hold two fingers below the reel, push the back bar and cast to the front of the fish. You cast like you are playing tennis, with overhand, underhand, forehand and backhand, whatever to get in front of the fish. A six to ten pound snook is common in The Keys, a ten to sixteen pound is a prize. In the Bahamas, they are closer to three pounds."

A small shark swam around the boat and spooked the school of fish we were following on the mirror-flat water.

The guide continued, "The Keys are diverse. We are south of the Everglades so we benefit from the fresh flowing water coming from the Florida mainland. A lot of people take seriously the eco system and how quickly this Nirvana could all disappear. So, here it's up to 20 feet deep, then 3 miles out it drops to 100 feet, then 10 miles out the depth drops to 1,000 feet. So, extremely diverse marine life lives on this Gulf side. Then you know about the Atlantic side. I remember you were big fishermen from the Bahamas."

"Even though we are close to the Everglades, the alligators don't come here. They don't like the salt water. We see an occasional crocodile. The islands have some coral snakes and lots of black racers. Some 98 percent of our guests are U.S. citizens, most of them white. We don't get many foreigners interested in bone fishing," he continued as he poled us into a channel where the fish would float to us in the current.

We cast a few practice rounds. I had fished with my father, so it was like riding a bike, and came back easily.

"What is that family in that Wellcraft doing? Are they allowed to be diving for lobster here?" I asked.

"No, there are specific dates and places for lobster season and a

limit on how many per person," said the guide.
"Drive over there. I want to get their license," I requested.
Ted gave the guide a nod to listen to me.
"What are you guys doing? Looks like you are boating coolers full of lobster. You know you aren't allowed to do that here," I greeted as we pulled up beside the boat.
I had my pen and paper as always and noted, "Wellcraft license number xxxxHW."
The man pretended he didn't know any better and told the preteens to put the lobsters back in the water. They didn't. They just waited for us to pull away, and we could see them jumping back in with snorkels and fins to illegally rape the lobster population.
"People who bend or break the rules teach their children to break the rules, then the next generation has no respect," the ranger said as he waited to report to the Park Ranger on his cell phone.
The captain reported to us, "The Park Rangers are too busy to cover this whole water park. They said by the time they get to this spot, these criminals will likely be gone."
The guide entertained us as we caught and released 12 smaller fish. Mutton snapper and stingrays swam around the skiff.
"The tarpon are hard to catch and this smaller species is fun to catch. The tarpon spawn here April to June and some of our resident fish migrate to the Bahamas and Mexico. The barracuda are the only predators who hunt them," he continued as we pulled back into the dock.
I couldn't easily shake the image of the middle school lobster robbers. How were these young people to grow into responsible adults being taught the corrupt value system of the Wellcraft driver, presumably the father? Respect has to start with children and parents in the home life.
The lobsters are protected so the species is sustainable but only if people follow the rules. I wondered if our culture was sustainable. All the reading of my notes had me in a somber mood.

# CHAPTER 33
## WET DUET AND THE ART OF LISTENING

"This place is insanely busy again," I noted as we checked into Cheeca Lodge in Islamorada.

"Somehow the traditional island vibe you expect in the Keys clashes with the Disney-like frenzy of Cheeca," whispered Ted.

"When Owen docked Blue Daze here last year it was a whole different experience than checking into the resort," I whispered back.

"We've upgraded you to the superior cabin," beamed a perspiring cheery face behind the rattan desk.

"Not surprising! Cat gets us upgrades every time we check in to hotels. It's uncanny statistically how often she gets TSA pre-check and penthouse upgrades," Ted moped.

"Don't be competitive. My positive energy benefits you, too," I said.

Ted was talking in code about some bimbo he met. I pretended, like I always did, that I didn't make the mental connection. We got organized in the superior cabin and I took a quick shower. In the shower, I heard Y, 'Remind him who you are.' Then the concert started. The chill bumps tickled up my arms. In operatic sense-around sensation the song "Ave Maria" filled the small wet space. When spiritual messages are sent through lyrics, I feel, not simply hear. Sometimes the lyrics are with songs that are playing. This time, the song was in my head. I heard it start with a man's voice and then a woman joined in for a duet. I hopped out of the shower and haphazardly wrapped a towel around my dripping body. Ted was on his iPad reading e-mails.

"Ted, quick, get on YouTube and play 'Ave Maria' by Pavarotti. I'm getting a message. I think someone has died," I said.

I heard Y, "Twice."

"Why," procrastinated Ted.

In his haste, I played the song on my iPhone.

The Latin lyrics filled the suite, "Dominus tecum, Benedicta tu in mulieribus ..."

"The song is from Luke when the angel tells Mary that God is with her and that she is blessed among women," I mumbled as the song bellowed from my small device.

"Cat, Owen's best friend George has died. Owen sent an e-mail to all of us. Did you see this yet?" said Ted glued to his iPad.

"No, that's terrible. I'm so sorry. So, this message perhaps is from George? I was trying to make lunch plans with George recently to ask him about Light International. Remember the Unlucky-13 Stalker said he was involved in this international business group? I knew that George had knowledge of it, so I was trying to meet with him. Don knew, too, but he died of a heart attack last year before we could meet," I pondered totally ignored by Ted.

"This is another miracle. How do you know these things? How can you predict these things? It makes me a little afraid of you," admitted Ted.

"I'm not like Whoopi Goldberg in 'Ghost' or Samantha in 'Bewitched.' I'm just a good listener. And I obey," I responded.

I didn't tell him about the "Twice" directive in the spiritual message. There was no need for alarm that a female passing was also at hand.

I hit replay to play "Ave Maria" twice.

We had a simple dinner at Chef Michael's a few blocks away.

"So, how do you know these things? Teach me how to know what you know," grilled Ted.

"I have to be really careful about my interpretations of messages. I know when I'm getting a message, but I don't always have full understanding right away. Remember when my old boyfriend Roger came to me in a vision and he wouldn't leave? I could sense clearly that it was he, but he was so giddy and silly unlike the normal intellectual serious business man. I finally gave him my attention and he waved and blew me a kiss, again unlike the man. I was concerned so I called his daughter-in-law. She said that he didn't die the previous week when I had the vision but that was his wedding day. He married. He didn't die. He said goodbye because he was marrying," I explained.

"I don't like it when you talk about your old boyfriends," Ted grumbled.

"It's just an example of using discernment in applying spiritual messages," I said as he cut me off and addressed our server.

"I'll have two scotches, one Macallan 12 and one Glenmorainge in honor of my friend George," Ted directed the server.

We took photos of ourselves with our three drink toast, two scotches and a chard. Ted withdrew into himself as he sipped on the tan elixirs. In great depth, he compared the lighter and darker colors of the two while he remembered our long-time friend. He was sad. His eyes watered. The scotches represented the two friends.

To entertain myself, I photographed the island fare for my social media posts.

I turned the camera so Ted could see the playback panel.

"George photo-bombed all of our photos tonight. Look at these orbs! See the dots on all the photos?" I asked.

"That could just be the light or something wet got on the lens," he pushed back.

"Hi George!" I greeted as I gazed up to the starry sky over the Atlantic, "So good to hear from you tonight!"

I picked a twinkling star in the dark dusk expanse and made my standard wish.

A crashing of glass brought my focus back to the table. Ted laughed as he dabbed up the wine he spilled.

"Remember when we were at Agape Substance in Rive Gauche at the community table and I knocked wine into that guy's dinner twice? We just arrived in Paris all jet lagged and my drinks just kept splashing his way," reminisced Ted with his cheeks pink from his scotches.

"We thought it was funny, but he sure didn't. That young couple probably saved forever to afford such an expensive special occasion dinner. Then to his dismay, he sat by the bad American!" I laughed.

"I've spilled my share of fine scotches," noted Ted.

"The worst was when a wine glass toppled through the gold bars of the bannister in the The Rose Club at The Plaza. Oh my! It dropped to the first floor to the Palm Court with a boom on the tile floor. Thankfully the jazz music camouflaged the snafu," I recalled.

"I spill fine wines, too. We sure have had some memorable times between the crystal crashes," he mused.

# CHAPTER 34
## GET OUT OF DODGE FROM CHEECA LODGE

As we sauntered past our private cabana downstairs from our cottage upstairs, it was obvious someone had entered our private space.

"Look Ted, someone has trashed our cabana! Someone had dinner here, a beer drinker, and left their trash. They left a wet towel in our hammock and footprints all over. Both yuck and creepy," I said as my voice got higher.

"The front desk just told us they can't control where people go," Ted said shaking his head after he called to ask them to send someone to clean up the mess.

"Really, that was the response? Can you please check to make sure the door is locked?" I asked as I peeked outside all of the windows.

"You are safe with me Cat," he assured.

What he didn't realize is that as he was preoccupied with the trashed private patio, I picked up a handwritten note in a baggie labeled, "To CAT" and had tucked it in my backpack. I went into the bathroom and stared in the mirror. I reluctantly pulled the white paper from the plastic bag.

The note read, "You aren't reading my notes in the iPhone. This is important Charlotte. Time is of the essence. I have information fit for a queen, LaReign."

LaReign was my mother's middle name. It meant "the queen" in French.

"He's done his research," I thought, "But what does he want with me?"

I ripped the note, tossed it in the toilet, and flushed it. As I watched the swirling water engulf the evidence, I meditated. I visualized The Fugitive being washed out of my life in a riptide.

I texted J, "Are you reading the notes?"

J texted back, "No. I peek at the iPhone but haven't touched it. I think the battery is dead anyway. I'm on the boat now. Someone has been in the engine room again."

I texted, "OK, don't read notes. I'm getting notes here. Creepy! More to come. Contact Ed about the boat issues. Thank you!"

# CHAPTER 35
## LITTLE TORCH BIG FLAME

The morning heat beat down on us as we got back in the car.

The radio started with the Gin Blossoms, "I want to tell if I am or am not myself, it's hard to know, how far or if at all could go? I've waited for far too long ..."

"You know, if your friend hadn't lied the night I met you and told you that she was dating me, we likely would have ended up together sooner," said Ted.

"She obviously wasn't a friend. We were at Black Fin and she was being a manipulative single woman, I just didn't know the rules. I didn't know you can't trust some other women when it comes to men," I said.

"You know, it's curious to me, because we have ended up together anyway, it was just delayed a few years," I said.

"But, you know, together the way you really want, married. I think about Little Palm Island as a destination-wedding venue and that is what you deserve. I could have gotten married a few years back, but I'm just not going to now. And when we first met, and you were supposed to meet three guys, I really should have introduced you to my single friends," he said.

"You introduced me to them as your girlfriend. Hello. I think you are saying something nice, but it's not feeling nice on my insides," I said.

I changed the subject, "What's up with all the dump trucks going north? Multiple company logos on the sides, but a hundred have passed us. Bizarre."

"Probably human trafficking bringing illegals into the country. Maybe they are equipped with air conditioning in the back. Think about it. Key West is closer to Cuba than Miami. You have all these small sparsely populated islands for immigrants to raft up to. If they make it to a U.S. coast, we let them in. I've seen dead bodies floating out there of ones who haven't made it when I'm fishing. The U.S. has a strong allure for people in other countries," Ted speculated.

An hour and a half later, after miles of islands, bridges, clouds and conversation along U.S. Highway One, at Mile Marker 28.5, we spotted the sign for Little Torch Key. We drove on Pirate Road to the parking lot with the large thatched roof reception center to the 5 acre 30 suite island resort.

Ann texted as we pull in, "omg. The skinny glam bartender at New Year's committed suicide. Shocking."

Ted sneered, "Antsy needs a life. What is up with her now? Good thing cell phones aren't allowed on the island so tune her out for a while."

I turned my phone off. I didn't have a response for such sad news. People should never get to such a painful place that they take their own life. She was such a pretty girl. I recalled that she asked us for help. She told us she was spent. We weren't very good listeners.

"Welcome back," the bellman smiled and handed us Gumby Slumber red rum punches. We checked in quickly and got aboard The Truman, a small polished dark wood antique shuttle yacht. We splashed along 15 minutes to the private island.

Our concierge checked us in to our cottage with a pitched roof, thatched inside and out. A wood plaque with Scrabble-like wood letters said "CAT" on our cottage. Ted didn't like to use our real last names like the other cottages. The purpose of privacy made no sense to announce who you are. The warm wood floors and the British West Indies furnishings of mahogany and bamboo softened with colors of the sea and champagne resembled my own décor in my home. I felt at home here. The oversized four-poster bed was high with wood step stools on either side. The sitting area offered no electronics, no TV, but it did have two books, "The DaVinci Code" and "Hannibals."

Outside, gardeners meticulously raked the white sugar sand on the pathway outside of our cottage and laid cypress mulch in the plant beds. We winded around the sand pathways lined with coquina rock and the freshly laid cypress mulch.

"The mature sea grapes and hibiscus and other tropical plants aren't that much different than what we have in Florida, but how they have made it seem like Gilligan's Island here is remarkable," I noted.

"Remember when we stayed in the cottage at the Four Seasons in Santa Barbara?" he asked as he looked around at the manicured landscaping.

"We had the best manicured landscaping of all of the cottages, the lawn guys didn't leave our vicinity. We must have put on quite a show for our landscapers with our music, jokes and shenanigans. For several days, every time we walked out, they were right there by our door," he laughed.

Unlike me, Ted liked attention. He liked attention from me. He liked attention from everyone in the room to notice that I was giving him attention. He had an insatiable male ego.

We walked to the pool for an early lunch. Ted brought the binoculars and the waterproof guide to birds of south Florida. We walked over to the docks along the bird sanctuary. A gentle sea cow floated under the dock.

"The sanderlings are the small gray shore birds chasing the waves up and back on the beach. There is a heron wading and look at the roseate spoonbill," he pointed to a speck of feathers to our left.

"Did you know the common white pelican is the second largest flying bird in North America? There is a falcon here, too, a small teal one," he whispered as he rotated the binoculars around the horizon.

We went for a swim in the pool and had lunch at the Palapa Bar, the poolside tiki bar.

He pulled a wet $10 bill from his baggies. He had a man-crush on Alexander Hamilton.

"Alexander Hamilton was a good-looking man," he said and pointed to the soggy bill, "He loved his wife and kids but married a hooker that took him down. He was a bastard and went back to his sordid roots. His mother was always with different guys and not married when he was born. He was an amazing writer with this flowery style that he wrote to the government in New York when Washington was president. You know the government started in New York. Hamilton was the Secretary of the Treasury, and really ran the U.S. He set up the first bank, established the coast guard, set up the bond trading market and assumed debts for states. He was an avid reader and became Washington's main aide. His forte was that he was a good writer."

He brought his attention back to me after his monologue, "He was a good writer, but you will be the best writer of all time."

"The message in your $10 bill, is that we all have value, we all have something to offer, and sometimes it is surprising who will rise to the top. Any individual can change a country, or the world," I offered.

We wrapped towels around our wet swimsuits and sat at the poolside tables and ordered fish tacos and Key Lime pie.

"I've got a sugar crash now. To Little Palm Island's slogan of 'get lost' add be a sloth, a honey sloth," he mumbled.

"Look the mojitos have cocoanut water in them, so actually they are healthy," I said with a big, "mmmmmmm."

"I'll have what she's having," he laughed and threw back his head and gestured like the line in the film "When Harry Met Sally."

By the activity tent, a chalkboard announced the important news of the day, "Wind E 5-10, Temp 85-78, Sunset 8:08."

We walked by the two docks of private boats and two private seaplanes and booked the snorkel trip mid-afternoon. Looe Key National Marine Sanctuary, a 200 by 800 yard live reef lies 4 miles due south of the resort, just 10 minutes in the resort's dive boat.

"I like that they take us to the reef with a boat and captain and wait for us. It's convenient to have the towels and waters and everything taken care of. When we boat on your boat, we have so much more to think about than just snorkeling. The reef here is one of the most alive and vibrant reefs we have explored, and we've been to a lot of islands," I exclaimed as we changed into our swimsuits.

We had the boat to ourselves. We had a little chop in the water so it took 15 minutes to get to the coral reefs. A hundred or so boats tied up to the moorings around the reef, along with our boat.

The captain offered us baby shampoo to clear our masks and put the ladder down for us to climb into the ocean. We attached the Velcro ends of the surf leash to our wrists so we could remain together as we swam.

Within seconds, we were in a magical other-world. We saw blue tang, little neon yellow schools of fish, sargent majors, pink jelly fish, about 20 barracudas, and 2 reef sharks.

A four foot barracuda parked itself between the reef and the ladder of the boat. Ted pulled on the leash to get my attention, pointed to the predator, and chopped his thumb and fingers together like an alligator puppet to signal, "Danger, something wants to eat you."

We circled back to the reef several times to wait for the barracuda to move. He stayed. We finally swam around him and safely climbed into the boat.

"Did you hear the parrot fish crunching on the coral?" Ted asked as he shook the water out of his ears.

"That was spectacular snorkeling," I said.

The guide said, "Now I'm going to take you to the western end of this dive spot at Looe Key. We call it the Wild West. The underground canyons open to the open ocean so larger marine life circle through here on their way migrating through the islands."

We splashed back in the water at Wild West. In short order I was tugging on the leash to get Ted's attention. We were about 20 yards from the boat in one of the canyons and sharks, sharks plural, were headed our way. Big sharks. Possibly hungry sharks from migrating. Possibly sharks that didn't understand the rules of safe little Looe Key. I started snapping photos with my new underwater camera. One curious carnivore swam right up to us, only five feet away, then at the last minute, dove under our feet and to our other side. I had photos of the whole ordeal. I didn't need to pull the leash to get Ted swimming back to the boat. When we were just 20 feet away, I looked down and here was the same shark circling back towards us, coming up from the bottom of the sandy canyon floor. I jumped in the boat within seconds. My swim team training of my youth came in handy in water related predicaments. Ted climbed up after me.

"You left me!" he pouted.

"I didn't leave you, I was in survival mode. We had to take turns getting on the ladder anyway," I said.

"I figured out the issue. Look at your new hip-cool camera. Some designer made it look like a fish. It's metallic blue and the lens looks like an eye and the handle is a tail," pointed out Ted.

"That's it! The shark was curious about this new marine delicacy. Things are not always as they appear. Sometimes we inadvertently attract fear and danger into our lives," I said.

## CHAPTER 36
## LITTLE PALM ISLAND SUNSET

An hour later, we were walking to dinner in a world-class, super luxury, private island but Ted was always planning the next best, bigger, better, more extravagant, more adventurous excursion.

"My buddy has a seaplane in Brevard County. Let's come by plane with him next trip. Or we can take a seaplane from Miami again," Ted suggested.

"Sunset celebration for today, our here and now, first! I hear the pianist warming up by the dining room," I said.

One of the few golf carts puttered by with heavy bags of ice.

We checked into the open-air dining room with white tablecloths, silver and crystal. We chose the adjacent al fresco dining area on the beach on the southwest tip of the island. We watched as they lit the Tiki torches. The servers were chasing away the key deer that inhabit the island along with the celebrities and seclusionists. A server threw water on one of the miniature deer. The deer defiantly stood between the teak tables placed between clumps of sea oats and sea grasses in the sand.

"The key deer have velvet racks and antlers. Us tourists like to photograph them, but you know the hotel staff would like hunting season," he remarked.

A few other couples were already seated, all wearing the latest resort wear and accessories. Little Palm Island is a romantic celebratory spot, so I assume many of the couples are there for anniversaries. Some of the couples had walked out to the dock where The Truman had dropped us off earlier. The shuttle journeyed back to the mainland every 15 minutes.

A boatload was unloading for the dinner. They looked more like they were from Miami than Little Palm Island. The dresses were short and the heels high. The men had long hair and the women short tempers. One yapped as they got off the boat at her man in an annoying screech you could hear from the beach. I was relieved when they, of course, chose to sit on the veranda rather than beach side by us. They weren't dressed for the beach.

We had another rum drink just because that is what you do on an island. Hugs and kisses filled the island tip as 8:08 p.m. as the tangerine sun set over the lilac-colored mainland. The couples who were still in love, about half, gave heartfelt kisses to their mates.

"Why is that guy trying to get your attention and why are you avoiding him?" I asked Ted.

A pock and scar faced man glared with deep-set black eyes. He had a bad haircut with loose unruly curls too long past his shirt collar. He wore a tacky polyester tropical print shirt and wrinkled white pants. A classless redhead tapped her fake acrylic nails on her iPhone ignoring the man. She was online shopping and sharing her online finds in a loud voice to her dinner date.

Ted pretended he didn't know him at first and then realized the tight quarters and small sticky social situation and confessed, "He was at an investor meeting in Miami. He's running a massive medical marijuana operation that is coming to Florida."

"I'm totally anti-drug. I think this whole idea will be abused by people who look something like that guy," I snapped, then went silent.

He had already made the decision and it was his investment funds, so I didn't have a say. Besides that, why wreck our getaway? I kept my full opinion to myself.

I ordered the local snapper and Ted the grouper. They served the fresh fish filets with Caribbean influences like mango and citrus. I started with the rich crab bisque.

"In a place where everyone is in swimsuits all day, it's really a conundrum that the menu is so tasty," I joked.

"Don't worry. I intend to help you work off those calories," he flirted.

"This is the most romantic of all of our getaway spots. I'm so happy to be here with you again," I oozed.

"You and I can come here for a few days which is perfect. For couples who come for a whole week with no TV or phones, I'd have to spice it up. Add naked Twister games with costume rentals and maybe a porn flick on the lawn. How about a nude beach? Hookers would be a fun touch," he teased.

He probably really thought of those ideas, but I was the girlfriend, not one the bad girls. Instead we got ice cream desserts to take back to our room.

"Oh my God," I exclaimed as I pointed to two large dead brown palm fronds placed on the steps to our cottage.

"So, what?" said Ted, "Just move them."

"No, they were placed there. There are no palms around here, look around. There are a man's bare footprints all over in the freshly raked sand, even going to our window. This is so creepy," I said with my voice shaking, and my head spinning in all directions.

"Look Cat, you've got to stop being fearful. There is nothing at all to be afraid of here. Nobody can get on or off of this island, it's private," he said calmly as he looked in all directions.

"There is an ocean and a shoreline, anyone can pull up in a small boat, or a kayak, or swim or snorkel up, or just ride on The Truman," I argued.

"Anyone can get anywhere, but you are with me and you are safe," he said as he tossed the dried palm fronds into the sea grape bushes.

I didn't want to argue with Ted. I wanted him to be right. But he wasn't. While he tossed the palms, I picked up a Baggie with a note in it. I put it in my Eric Jarvis straw purse with the turquoise starfish clasp. The note barely fit. I wanted the note and the note writer to swim away and leave me alone. I visualized him in the water in a rip tide. I went to the bathroom to read the note.

This note read, "Check your Notes. I have a laptop for you with documents that you will find helpful. It's for the Finger family. Like the Michelangelo's finger on the Sistine Chapel, you will find these small details of great interest."

I stared frozen at the note. On my mother's side, my grandmother's maiden name was Finger. They were early American colonists, dairy farmers from Scotland.

Again, I ripped and flushed the evidence and flushed The Stalker.

"Everything OK in there?" asked Ted.

"Sure. I'll be right out," I said as I brushed my hair and put on Barbie pink lipstick.

The turn down service had drawn the white mosquito netting around the bed, and left a postcard with a small nightlight attached to it. Tonight's message I read aloud to Ted, "What will be, will be."

Ted turned on his iPad and a tinny bad reception played Pandora from the 1980s love songs channel.

"Well, here we are again, it must be fate ..." sang a scratchy version of the tune "After All" by Peter Cetera.

Ted's seduction started when he saw you. He'd raise his eyebrows and look you up and down and then compliment your looks. He'd notice if you had a haircut or were wearing a new outfit. "Beautiful," would flow from his lips. And then he'd offer a kiss on the lips, not French kiss, but tender and sweet. Then he'd present a gift. It might just be a bottle of wine or an announcement of an upcoming trip. He was Santa Claus. And then he touched my hand or shoulder or anywhere really throughout time until it was time to throw off our clothes. He had animal instinct of hunter-gatherer physical relationship perfected.

From all the day-drinking he fell asleep right away. I laid on the white down luxury bedding and stared for hours at the spinning bamboo-leaf ceiling fan. Ted woke up and checked the door and looked out of the windows about every hour. I pretended I was asleep. I avoided confrontation as much as I could. I didn't like confrontation.

The ice cream we brought back to the villa melted un-touched. In this bliss something was amiss.

# CHAPTER 37
## KEYS TO HAPPINESS

We split a Cuban sandwich for breakfast. I'm not much of a breakfast food fan. The cappuccinos helped relieve the hangovers. We sat in our robes on the patio partially made private with tropical foliage.

I peeked and all evidence of the bare feet was gone, but so were our footprints. The sand was neatly raked.

From our patio table, Ted spotted shark fins. He had an eagle eye on the water from all of his fishing. He didn't point out the sand, but he missed little so I knew he had made a mental note. He also pointed out the choppy water and noted our morning dive would likely be cancelled. It was.

I turned up the crystal chandelier lamp by the full-length mirror by the bed as I put on my two-piece. I didn't look like the leggy Vogue-like recent college grad with the old guy who sat next to us at dinner. At least everyone had dinner but her. I noticed she had a dressing-less salad and picked at grilled fish. She looked bored ... Starving and bored. In the mirror, I looked 50-ish, maybe 40-ish. I had some cellulite around my abdomen and thighs. I put on a sarong around the fashion imperfection and pulled my hair into a ponytail.

The bellman got our bags and The Truman yacht motored us back to the parking lot on the mainland and the welcome center. The blonde and her sugar daddy were checking out, too. She bought two bags of clothes in the gift shop. She had three suitcases. Not much more would have fit on the small vessel, so it was good only the four of us were leaving that morning. The waters were calming down, but we had already checked out. We had a short drive to Key West and had now booked a charter boat to snorkel the reefs there.

The radio sang "Garden Party" by Ricky Nelson from 1970s, "I learned my lesson well, ya' can't please everyone so ya' have to please yourself ..."

I shifted energy from bliss to burdened as I clicked on the iPhone. I had lots of texts from Ann.

I first responded to Ann's texts about the bartender who died, "Play Ave Maria. Will make you feel better about this loss. More on this when we talk."

"The second Ave Maria message was a Palm Beach bartender who committed suicide. I heard a duet with a woman's voice. I knew there were two soul passings but I didn't want to alarm you," I told Ted.

He didn't respond. I didn't repeat it. By the time I answered my e-mails and texts and read all of Ted's e-mails to him from his iPad, we were pulling into the Pierhouse at on Duval Street in downtown Key West.

"Little Palm Island is a little fun, but Key West is party central," Ted beamed as the valet approached us.

We ordered lobster sliders on Hawaiian rolls with mango aioli with Caribbean coleslaw at One Duval next door. The live acoustic guitar bobbed on a wood stool as he sang Bob Marley's "Three Little Birds," "Don't worry about a thing 'cause every little thing gonna' be alright..."

Navy ships with soldiers in wetsuits sailed by from the Navy base on the island and Ted pointed out, "You don't want to mess with those guys. The Navy Seals are the best weapon in all of America."

We drove to Sunset Marina for our private snorkel charter. The captain of the small skiff took us 20 minutes to the coral heads of Man Key. They were bland and ho-hum compared to the colorful Looe Key.

We climbed back in the boat and I said, "I saw a bunch of starfish. I saw a sawfish for the first time."

He said, "We don't like to tell people the sawfish are here because they try to kill them."

"What is up with human nature? In Islamorada we witnessed pure greedy scumbags loading their boat with illegal lobsters," I said.

"Passionate people have to protect our national treasures. And I'm not just talking about the fish. Ten people have gone missing in The Keys so far this year. And look what our Seals have to protect with just a handful of them," Captain shook his head.

Captain took us to a few more dive spots. We saw a sea turtle. A barracuda followed us. We got in the boat when we saw a shark. It was a ditto dive like many we had done.

We dressed for an early happy hour. We did a dock walk around A&B Marina two blocks away. Chickens were running on the concrete floors in and out of the open-air casual restaurants along the marina.

"Remember when I kept Sunny at this marina last year? That was a blast," said Ted.

We walked into the Schooner Wharf Bar with the sand floor, salty smokers, and live music on stage. The sweaty loony locals congregated in a circle around the end of the bar and talked about the weird tourists. They obviously had not looked in the mirror in a while. A gritty male voice boomed over the speakers, over the slurred drunken conversations, Jimmy Buffet's song, "Why don't we get drunk and screw?"

We walked back to Duval to Sloppy Joe's to watch the tourists ourselves, but not with disdain like the salty locals, but more with curiosity and an open mind for fun.

Ted requested "The Wreck of the Edmund Fitzgerald" by Gordon Lightfoot to the live singer / guitarist, who started then quickly gave up and made up lyrics, "The legend lives on from the Chippewa on down, of the big lake they call 'gitche goomee' ... something something wrecked and the captain and crew and the man they call Ted was a-drinkin' ..."

"No musician could remember all those lyrics. Especially since they sit up there and drink beer all day between songs," laughed Ted.

"You obviously have requested it before and he even added your name to his version of the song," I pointed out.

"Well, you know I was here last winter and Captain Ed had Owen's Blue Daze on the dock next to me. It was a par-tay," he rubbed in my face.

He noticed my body language and reminded me, "You were here, too."

"For one weekend," I clarified, "I don't like that you two were here for Fantasy Fest, especially without me. Anyway, we are together here now so let's enjoy the music."

A bachelor party of young men came in and sat beside us. Ted bought a round of whiskey shots for them. Ted loved to serve up the life of the party.

We freshened up back at Pierhouse and walked next door to Sunset Pier at Ocean Key Resort at Zero Duval Street. The sunset crowd grew below us to fill Mallory Square with artists, jugglers, tourists, partiers, and hippies that lost themselves in Key West. We watched the setup of the limbo contest, the silent live Statue-of-Liberty actor, and the Calypso band. Body painted women ran by us, one painted as Super Woman and one as a cheetah. It didn't look like they had on any clothing under the paint.

The four-piece band played the Righteous Brothers' song "Unchained Melody," "Lonely rivers flow to the sea, to the sea ... All alone I gaze at the stars, at the stars, dreaming of my love far away ..."

I felt guilty. I felt lonely. Here I was with the love of my life, and he was more interested in the weird characters than in me. He was entertained by, or moreover, entertaining to the crowd.

The sun set. The crowd cheered.

Ted looked at me and said, "You know what the key to happiness is? Know happiness is only here and now. And you make me happy, Cat."

"It's easy to be happy here in Key West. Happy follows you because you are a walking party," I smiled.

All I could think is this man is so handsome and how could I ever live without him. I'm sure lots of women think that about their men. I'm sure it's rarely true. Although, my mother died right after my dad. She really couldn't live without him. She passed on the "romantic gene" to me, rose-colored glasses and all.

We took a ten minute golf cart shuttle to the Southernmost Hotel for another cocktail, which we did not need. We walked two blocks to Louis' Backyard for alfresco dinner by the ocean. I could barely remember what I ordered after all the libations.

On the walk back to the hotel, we caught the karaoke bar before it closed. I sang Faith Hill's "Lost" only for a few lines then gave up. My voice has grown raspy as of late.

Once again, a plastic bag with a note inside was left by our hotel room door. Ted was intoxicated and didn't notice. I secretly picked it up. He fell asleep right away again. I sat on the edge of the bed with the drapes still open. The full moon reflected off of the sea like shimmering Christmas lights. Outside didn't look so ominous. But someone outside could be harmful to me. I didn't understand why this Fugitive was following me. Why didn't he just walk up and talk to us?

I read the note, "So, you can't read the notes because the iPhone is in the boat. When you get back, I have a laptop for you. It will have KOAD. The history is the mystery to you."

I contemplated his note and read it out loud, "KOAD? Code? Code to what? He's giving notes about my mother's middle name and her mother's maiden name ... and Doak. That is a family name on my mother's side a few generations back. He's going back a few generations each note. What is he trying to tell me? Or is he just stalking me and being a nuisance? Maybe he is insane and I really should go to the authorities. I've destroyed all the evidence, so I'm really at a loss of what to do."

I slowly walked into the bathroom. I read the note three more times before I disposed of it in what now was becoming a familiar ritual. I ripped it up, flushed it, and flushed the energy of The Fugitive out of my life. I visualized a vicious riptide.

I walked back to the window to close the drapes. I found a star. I made a wish. I wished the same wish as always. I wanted a family.

# CHAPTER 38
## SIMPATICO

We slept in then wandered a block south of Duvall to Whitehead Street past the historic 1800s homes, Truman's Little White House and the Audubon House. In the Green Parrot bar, four homeless looking alcoholics had already bellied up to the bar.

"At the Green Parrot, the early bird gets the worm, or better yet, just never leave!" laughed Ted.

The Hemingway House museum wasn't open yet so we stopped at the Six-Toed Cat café for breakfast. I asked for the lunch menu. We both ordered a Reuben.

"We are so in sync. I find it uncanny that we both order the same meals! We have the same sleep schedules, enjoy the same activities, politically agree, similar health habits ... do you know how unique we are that we found each other?" I asked.

"It's because we spend so much time together," he surmised.

"Well, I've spent time with men in the past and never clicked like this, so it's not just time, we fit," I said.

"You are my soulmate. You are also my little Ernie. Ernest Hemingway has nothing on my little writer. You've done all of those hunting and fishing 'guy' trips. You fish and hunt better than most men. You aren't the four Hemingway wives, not that there's anything wrong with that. You are the feminine version of Hemingway. Ernie! That is you," he smiled.

"Well, you complete Ernie. Whom would I do all those adventures with if you weren't in my life?" I gave him credit.

"It was just such a fun few days Ernie. I don't know one other girl who would want to do all that. I don't know one who could. I certainly don't know one who would enjoy it as much as you. I don't know anyone female or male who enjoys life as much as you," flattered Ted.

"What do you mean? Because I like the hunting and fishing and water sports?" I asked.

"That for sure separates you from other girls. Others like to spa. You want to be in the action. You are also a foodie, so fine dining is enjoyable with you. And nobody is more humorous to drink with. And you are smart, so conversation is stimulating. I talk to you about business and you have intelligent insights. Sweet. You are always sugar sweet. You are my girlfriend and my best friend in one person," he said.

We walked past the strutting roosters wandering the streets.

"Remember the courting Bahamian roosters in Harbour Island? Pink Sands was full so we stayed at Coral Sands. We watched the rooster strut all over the large courtyard behind the villa. The chicken pranced around teasing him. Then pounce! The rooster shot across the grass and that chicken got some," said Ted.

"What is up with the promiscuous roosters in all of these islands?" I asked being silly.

The trolley cars were still running empty. Key West was still asleep as we packed to head north to Fort Lauderdale.

I didn't worry Ted with the notes. I flushed them both physically and mentally. Whatever The Fujitive was trying to tell me, was of no interest to me. I didn't want to know. I wanted him to leave me alone. He was in Key West now known for wayward misfits who find themselves at the Southernmost Point of the U.S., the end of the line. I assumed he might be comfortable in just such a spot and stay there. Luckily for me that theory might have been true, at least for a while the notes would stop.

# CHAPTER 39
# GROWING GUIDANCE IN YOUR GARDEN

I was back in Winter Park. I was back to my routine for a short while. It was early spring, my favorite Florida season.

I hear my inner guidance in nature. If the beach or mountains aren't convenient, my garden provides a fertile mecca for meditation. My ideal home would have a view of both mountains and coastline. There is a certain sense I get in Carmel or along the coastline in France, Italy or Scotland that inspire my writing. I visited Alfred Lord Tennyson's Isle of Wight home. I saw English families visiting the monument above the chalky limestone cliffs and reciting his poetry together. There was this incredible sense in that space for the need for fresh timeless messages. There are rumors of haunted library in Farringford and I had added it to my to-do list to go back.

This Sunday morning, I was praying about the ad agency. I had spent the last four months pitching a project to a previous client that was only supposed to last three months. It felt overwhelming. I suffered from insomnia the whole week as the pitch was to culminate with the signing of the agreement and Y was still giving me a "no." I self-directed the agenda from the beginning of the pitch because of my bank balance. I wanted the fee. I hadn't listened to Y. As a predictable result, I had a cyclone of inner turmoil.

Outside, the lilac, deep purple, white and pink azaleas bloomed like cotton candy on rich green shrubs. The oak canopy dropped leaves like snow giving movement from the sky to the pastel puffs of petals swaying in the spring breeze. From my Saturday garden gathering, I emptied a bounty of Winter Park Farmer's Market premium sunflowers, geraniums and herbs from my car to the front lawn.

My pre-dawn vision and verbal cue from Y was, "Garden. Start at the corner of Park Avenue."

I didn't plan to put my palette of spring hues anywhere but in my planters. "No, corner of Park Avenue," I heard inside very directly. Obediently, I walked to the corner of the yard.

Floating on top of the border grass in the corner was a five-tipped leaf. It was lit like a spotlight was aimed at its' brown flesh. I picked it up and heard, "Let go gently."

My body tingled all over as it does when Spirit is near. I looked in all directions in the earthly world. There was no tree in sight to produce that leaf. The neighborhood canopy grew oak, camphor, magnolia and crepe myrtles.

"Let go gently" is a title of a page of spiritual messages of a short book I wrote titled "Lessons of a Falling Leaf."

I was in the same receptive spiritual zone now as I had been when I wrote the leaf book in a spa in Buenos Aires one spring, which was fall in South America. I was alone as usual. Ted was with the guys.

I meditated further. The oak roots were growing to the surface choking out the nandina or heavenly bamboo hedge. I replaced the starved out nandinas with bromiliads with shallow roots. As I plopped down potting soil and pruned brown leaves and blooms, I heard from Y, "The dead saps from the living so trim what is no longer useful."

The second message affirmed the first message.

I asked again and Y communicated, "It's a choice. Go with a sure thing, or the thing that you are sure of. Destiny. Choice. Step out in faith. The time is near."

And with that I had a vision of a close up of a $20 bill with the words, "In God We Trust."

I primped my spring flowers in my pots.

I came in to check e-mails and my client had cancelled my meeting where we were going to sign the contract, and postponed the entire project. I wasn't surprised. I wasn't disappointed. I was relieved. I was spiritually prepared. The four months were not wasted. The project was not meant to be. That part of my advertising career no longer served my present, like the dying heavenly bamboo in the yard. I wanted the earthly reward, the fee. I pushed back against my intense internal insights, but, alas, fate wins every time over forced desires.

Inside, I fired up the Mac, and let go gently to my advertising client. I was incredibly grateful for all the past work he had given for me to support myself and my children. That season had passed. The work being offered no longer served me. It was not my destiny.

I felt peaceful, purposeful, and loved. Not logical but to walk in a state of knowing is all I know how to live. I felt connected to a greater knowledge than my education or experiences or intellect can access. The advertising agency had morphed into a PR firm, then into a publishing company, then into a book promotions company. All those had purpose to get me to where I am now but not part of my future. Y had other plans for my time, my skill set, my heart and my life. My destiny was to be a significant writer of this time.

Ted called and remarked about my experience with the leaf, "You always take the high road. You never hurt anyone. Somehow you always get rewarded. In our business deals, sometimes you are the only one who benefits. It's nothing you manipulate, but how events turn out. I watch you be saint-like time and time again."

I said, "Others unknowingly hurt themselves with trying to push what is not to be. I cannot ignore Y. I have to live in integrity in sync with Spirit. My mission is to bring light to dark in every interaction. It's a practice of principle. Now we are in a paradigm shift. The secret is not control and manifest individual desires. We are all connected. The secret is to listen to Spirit, then allow destiny to develop around the vision given by the Divine. The secret is to accept spiritual gifts in a peaceful and purposeful manner. The secret is to invite in the events, people, and opportunities that help manifest the vision of what already is meant to be."

Ted asked, "Can you teach people to do what I witness you do?"

I answered, "I would like to. Have I taught you?"

Ted answered, "You have taught me what is possible. You have opened my eyes to a spirit world I knew nothing about."

"That is a start. You are my soul project," I smiled.

"I'm searching for what all 'Let go gently' means," and stopped the rest of my verbal thought.

Relationship rule number one is you can't un-ring a bell. In the quiet of my heart, I was preparing to let him go.

We were at the go or grow point. I was quite amicable in my relationship. The notes from my early-single readings which I had recently re-read said that I had a pattern of trying to please people and that I put pressure on myself to over-perform. That created unrealistic illusions of what I should achieve, what people around me should also achieve, and what my relationships should look like. I had always been an over-achiever. It's a trait of a leader. I was willing to choose love over leadership. At this point though, I was bending so many rules, in so very many ways, I was becoming unrecognizable to myself. The seeds of change were planted and fertilized by my intuition.

I came inside and penned a poem from my garden-side meditation:

The Rest

Pink camellias in my garden,
Azaleas in full fuchsia bloom,
In my head, I could be most anywhere,
Breathing with nature in my outside room.

A wide-winged majestic dragonfly
Fluttered from behind a palm.
A red cardinal keeping dutiful watch
Added to the realm of calm.

A crane pecked at a lizard.
A neighbor's cat napped with a purr.
Squirrels scampered around the mulch
Where sunflower seeds once were.

I walked and watered and puttered
And stood in amazement before the rose.
I am reminded of those before me
And how what one plants surely grows.

In my little space I wondered
What seeds that I shall sow.
And my gentle Voice inside me
Again urged the vision I was to go.

As I trimmed fragrant herbs in pots,
The great fear welled up inside me.
And my Voice said, "Look to that above.
What is that placed upon the tree?"

On an outer branch above my door
A bird had constructed a massive nest.
"So, you do your work as birds have done,
And I will do the rest."

"A promise was made for protection
With the soft whisper of a feather
Of the wings of one thousand angels.
Your work is blessed ... in any weather."

"And when you sense a drought
In your garden look to the sky.
And remember I am with you,
And with me, you will surely fly."

# CHAPTER 40
## CLOSET DESIRES, LET GO GENTLY

When I had my first meeting with that last client, I couldn't find my career clothes that morning. I wore a black polka dot cotton dress way too casual for a business pitch. I lived mostly in sundresses and bright beachy colors on cotton fabrics. Since the kids had gone to college, I filled every closet but without much organization. I had a favorite closet at any given time. I needed to make order of my life. My friend right before my pending divorce became public knowledge, took one look at my intensely organized laundry room and asked, "So, is there anything you want to tell me? I know this behavior from my mother. You start working on your inside chaos with your outside world."

I got online and ordered four metal industrial clothes racks. I ordered two six foot tall shoe racks and a dozen plastic boxes for ski clothes, sweaters and seasonal items. I emptied the furniture from one of the vacant bedrooms, put it in the garage for donation, and pulled out every piece of clothing in every closet. I found my conservative career dresses. Many still had price tags on them. I buried myself in shoes, swimsuits, ski suits, sundresses, and emotionless busy work as I continued my meditation.

So, I wasn't taking on the ad agency client. So how was I to spend my spring? What did Y have in store for me? I was quite astonished by the response I felt. I triple checked to make sure it was not another of my own self-directed desires. I listened to my inner voice. I listened to my body. I even pulled out a pendulum and got a yes answer. Y wanted me to make myself available to travel with Ted.

I named my room-size closet the Packing Room. I bought a supply of travel size toiletries and bought new luggage. I made sure my phone had the international package and that my credit cards didn't charge foreign currency exchange fees.

I pulled out a copy of my small paperback book "Lessons From A Falling Leaf," and put it in my suitcase so it's energy would be with me as I traveled.

I read the chapter "Let Go Gently" before I tucked the tiny book in the side pocket:

“The five-tipped leaf gracefully and without fanfare, released from the safety of the branch and his sentry of the nest. He closed his eyes, said a prayer, and gently released his hold from his tethered state.

Anticipation, exhilaration, and relief all blended to a dizzying flash of great emotion as he tugged loose from a final hold from the branch.

Freedom felt deserved. The allure of the aura proved greater than the security of the branch and the other leaves. He had always been on the outside ready to deflect the hard rain and shade from the harsh sun. He was the protector but this time was his.

The airborne adventure began. The leaves waved farewell and blew kisses of encouragement and sang a song of ‘wssssh’ in the gentle breeze.

One of his tips brushed against a feather. It felt soft. He had spent a lifetime protecting the nest, yet had never known the birds intimately; now he touched one ever so briefly. He smiled with tender satisfaction. The lullaby peep of the baby birds muffled quickly as gravity called his name and as the wind rushed into his ears as he took flight. He could hear only his inner voice cheering him on in the words of the wind, ‘be free to see.’”

I held the paperback in my right hand. I had the new five-tip leaf message from heaven in my left. My life in the moment was in balance. I once again was listening, and more importantly, trusting.

# CHAPTER 41
## IN LOVE PER SE

I took Y's advice and asked Ted, "Where are we going next?"

"Funny you should ask Ernie Cat, I want you to go to New York with me next week," he responded.

"You know holidays you are always busy with your traditional trips with Captain Ed or your sons or whatever. I'd like you to prioritize me the next few holidays, ok?" I added while I was on a roll.

"I can work on that," he said, as he always said, adding as he always did, "I'm going to make that up to you."

The Universe was in full motion, clicking together seamlessly.

New York was a favorite spot for us. Ted had business there and I savored the art and culinary scene. I wasn't going to be able to go if I was filming TV commercials, so the era of "Let go gently" was in full swing.

Ted and I had lunch at our favorite restaurant Marea, right on Central Park, where "60 Minutes" journalists and other celebrities often were to the left and right of us. He left for his meeting and I walked a block to the Shops at Columbus Circle in the Time Warner Center. On our trips, I often was solo as much as a duo. I met him for cocktails at the Mandarin Hotel's MO Bar on the 35th floor with sweeping views of the lush green park. While I waited for him, I ordered The Royal Tea with Ketel One Vodka, Pomegranate, Beet Juice, Lemon, Ginger, Oolong Honey.

I asked the pretty college age server, "Can you tell me about that statue?"

"I think it is Columbus or something," she mumbled.

"You look at it every day. It's the focal point of all of these windows. So, you know who Columbus is don't you?" I asked terrified of what her answer might be.

"Well, he was a pioneer or an early president or something. I think he was French, oh, I really don't know," she said.

"The statue at Columbus Circle is the center point where all the streets in Manhattan are referenced from north, south, east and west. As for Christopher Columbus, seems like you should know that. I was actually inquiring about the golden horse statue in the park behind where we see Columbus," I sighed to her.

"You must think I'm blonde. I wish I knew more," she said in a baby voice as she tilted her head to the side like a curious puppy.

"I'm not good at remembering details either so I don't think you are blonde. I do think you could show some interest in the world around you and in our history and get the gist of how we got here" I suggested.

"I don't like history. It's boring," she responded.

"There is power and safety in knowledge. Some other countries don't enjoy the privilege and freedoms that we have. You chose to live in New York. You chose to work here. You chose your education. You are a free woman which many, many women in the world would love to have your opportunity. Instead of perceiving yourself as blonde, you can be beautiful and bright at any time. Awareness is a choice," I lightly suggested.

"I just don't like to read," she responded.

Of course, she could watch online films or talk to people or any number of ways to gain knowledge. She was happy in her self-imposed blonde bubble. She floated back into the crowd in her mini-skirt uniform while I Googled the golden statue.

"You are the best-looking gal in all of New York today. You look stunning all tan in your white sundress and heels. I can't wait to take it all off," greeted my cheerful boyfriend, whispering the last of his flattery.

"Not much competition! I'm the only one not in a T-shirt and shorts and flip flops. The tourists are more casual in New York City this summer than in Key West!" I agreed.

"No shopping bags?" he inquired.

"I did a quick window shop. I didn't really see anything. I like visiting the 14 foot brass Botero statues of Adam and Eve. I got my art fix with that since I didn't have time for MOMA today," I said.

"You didn't get the shopper gene or the bitch gene. Amazing. No wonder my friends all try to steal you. We're right at about 100 percent on the girlfriend theft attempt by my boys," he smiled.

"Look, the white Italian Max Mara purse with the seagull print we bought in London matches perfectly. I am not really a shopper, but I am a buyer when I find something that suits me. So, also, in London we saw 'Motown the Musical.' Tomorrow here in New York, we'll see 'An American in Paris.' I think we have Broadway transatlantic dyslexia!" I mused.

"So, speaking of statues, our server doesn't know who Columbus is. In school, I wasn't a big fan of history classes, but at least I knew the basics. I remember history classes taught by retired military guys who wanted us to sit up straight. In college, I took Florida History before 1800. It was the only class that fit my schedule so I could work at the surf shop in the afternoons. When history enchanted me was at that same time, when I was taking documentary film classes. History came to life in 'Hearts and Minds' about the Vietnam War. The most compelling was Hitler's propagandist Leni Riefenstahl. Her images still haunt me. It was that film making class where I realized how important my career as a journalist could be. Powerful messages can change the outcome of history. Not all powerful messages are truthful. In our era now with social media, neither good nor evil can control the messages, the audience, or how history will be recalled," I rambled.

Ted had never dined at Per Se, so we walked to the Time Warner Center for a prix fixe $325 a person epicurean episode. I might not remember the names of Indian Chiefs of early Florida, but I recall every time I've dined at Per Se, and it's an evening to remember. We indulged in Chef Thomas Keller's luxe petite servings of oysters, caviar, duck foie gras, Bluefin tuna, sea scallops, quail breast, beef short rib, wagyu steak, and more I couldn't recall without reference to the photos in my iPhone.

We waddled across the circle to Trump International.

"The Tagliatelle with the hand shaved Australian black truffles was so decadent! I didn't notice the $125 supplement till I saw it on the bill," I said.

"The oysters and caviar had me at hello. I can see why it's Per Se, or in and of itself. What a unique experience. I'm in a calorie coma now!" he teased, as he threw his clothes on the side chair and laid on the king bed, holding his tummy.

"Oh, come on Edward, you can't let those calories take you down for the count," I whispered as I curled up next to him.

"Edward! What about Ted? I want you all the time. Nobody else," he snapped.

"I'm calling you by your full name Ted. Edward and Ted are both you. I can't believe how jealous you are ... and jealous of yourself no less. No more scotch for Ted or Edward," I said.

I wasn't kidding about the let's stop drinking. He wasn't kidding about the jealous streak. I brought it up the next day and he admitted he was really jealous. Jealousy paired with insecurity is death to a relationship. Now he was jealous of a mirage and I was insecure because of his flirting tendencies.

I thought about it later. I had been to Per Se several times with a former boyfriend. He was in the culinary elite and a friend of the chef. I didn't think of the former boyfriend while I was with Ted. I wanted to share with Ted something that was a world-class must-do. I was simmering in the spice of life with Ted while he was unbeknownst to me simmering in envy, unwarranted envy. I live fully in my present. I dine at the table set before me. Every day is a miracle and every meal is a feast.

The table was set. New travel arrangements were made as each trip ended. I jet-setted with Ted as my priority that season in my life. All the travel was like having dessert only. Sometimes you want a balanced diet. I was craving a balanced life. I missed my work. I missed being me. Being creative and getting paid to be creative was a big part of who I am. I occasionally still met with my client Owen.

# CHAPTER 42
## SOMETHING FISHY IN THE WATER

I met my client Owen of American Valor Corp. at Brazilian Dock at the Palm Beach City Docks. He was busy in the galley on his yacht Blue Daze organizing his tackle and looking under all the seats in the storage compartments. I scampered to the compartment under the second stair and grabbed the bag with the iPhone. I wrote a note to Owen saying, "Shhhh," and motioned for him to leave his phone on the counter. I left mine, too.

"You had a package at the Dockmaster's office. Let's go get it," I pretended just in case there were listening devices on the boat which I assumed there was.

We clomped down the aluminum docks and I unloaded my predicament, "The Fujitive guy from Port Lucaya dropped off an iPhone here. He's putting messages in the Notes app. I only read one. Because I wasn't reading the notes, he followed me to Costa Rica and The Keys with handwritten mysterious notes," I explained.

"Give me the iPhone and I'll have forensics done on it. I'll have this Fugitive individual neutralized," Owen said sternly.

"These wayward Snowden-wannabees think they have power with knowledge. Power comes with honoring knowledge, not abusing it for personal gain. Knowledge is a tool to be respected. These wannabees are attracted to you like bees to honey. We've talked about you being less social and more self-protective," he said in father-like fashion.

"I really did nothing to encourage this ghost of a character. He literally came out of the blue sky, or really, the deep blue sea. I don't know if he's trying to tattle on something or someone," I retorted.

Owen cut me off, "I'll handle it."

We didn't really have a package to pick up, so we got the mail and headed back to Blue Daze and boarded the boat.

I handed the plastic bag with the original note and the iPhone to my trusted confidant. I wrote the username and password on a piece of paper and tucked it in the bag.

"Captain Ed arrives later today. We need to get this boat out of the Lake Worth lagoon. Lake Okeechobee right next to us in the Everglades has a 300 square mile blue green algae bloom. It's killing the plants that are the natural habitat for fish and marine life. It's killing the fish. It's killing manatees. It hasn't killed the alligators, but it's killing their food source, so now they are attacking more pets and children. It's going to get worse. Alligators are adaptable to water and land. Their prehistoric predatory migratory instincts will keep them intact. Then there are these crazy Zika mosquitos. Then the damn whole state is sinking. Remember when we were all in Fort Lauderdale at the oncoming of one of the last hurricanes? The water fully covered Atlantic Avenue. We had to wait for low tide so we could drive out of Las Olas. The waves rolled ten blocks inland over the streets, all the way to the intercoastal," he said.

"Is everything OK?" I asked my normally even-keeled client.

"Everything is going to be OK with some work. We are going to start with moving this boat. I've got Captain Ed studying the movement of the algae mass. As of now, we plan to take it to Sailfish Marina," he instructed.

"I have a meeting here about an offshore surveillance project," said Owen.

"The submarine surveillance?" I asked.

"Yes, if an enemy brings a major explosive close to our Florida coastline, we're going to have a real problem. Not green algae or little black mosquitos but a big blue wall of water coming at us at high speed," said Owen.

His dialogue triggered in me a premonition, a recurring nightmare I had since I was a child. I got very quiet. I stayed introspective through dinner. Owen's energy was uncomfortable to be around.

The three of us met for dinner at Bice. We dined al fresco on the patio. The pelting rain of typical Florida afternoon and evening showers forced us to move inside. I ordered my favorite Caesar salad and Antipasti Mellanzane Alla Parmigiana.

"This front moves through tonight and we've got mirror glassy seas for tomorrow," said Captain Ed.

"Be sure to check the engine room. It's been unlocked a few times. I'm not sure how anyone is getting in there. Remember when we did the crossing to the Bahamas to West End with the engine on fire? Scary! It smelled of rotten eggs for an hour before we made shore. We were lucky we made it. Maybe we shouldn't bring the boat back to City Docks until we change the locks," I suggested.

"Keep it in shape. The boat's for sale," ordered Owen.

"Again? We just got this boat," whined Captain Ed who didn't have a filter.

We walked outside and it was still daylight. The sun doesn't set until 8:30 p.m. in the summer. Owen said goodbye and darted across the street and a large brown truck swallowed him up into the belly of the vehicle like watching Jonah and the whale. I assumed there was surveillance gadgetry rather than Amazon Prime packages inside. Owen and company could hide in plain sight in their brown mobile headquarters.

# CHAPTER 43
## TIDAL WAVE DREAM

Back in my guesthouse, I could not sleep. Owen's somber talk of offshore submarines with explosives triggered to life the nightmares.

The vision starts at the end of Worth Ave. in Palm Beach. I didn't know that was the place until the first time I visited the island. Overlooking the pristine beach, out of the blue, in the distance on the horizon, I see a mammoth tidal wave building and rushing towards the shore. Just as the wall of water hits shore, the brilliant colors fade to monochrome and all turns to slow motion. The vision becomes fuzzy like viewing through a steamy shower door. The deafening thunder of the tidal wave grows louder till it hits land, then everything becomes totally silent. In my dream, I can fly, so I fly maybe 30 feet above ground, up and down streets, over all the places in Florida that I've ever lived or visited. The scenes click like watching a slide show from community to community. I look down and see screams on the faces of the people as they run randomly from building to building, looking all around in confusion and intense terror. In slow motion, the giant wave washes through the buildings and down the streets. It's not really water, but more of a clear vaporous wave. Above the clouds, another thunderous noise presents the hooves of massive war horses in full armor. The beasts emerge climbing from a single foxhole in the clouds. From the hole, the warriors of the ages, dressed in full battle gear, sprint up and run in all directions as far as the eye can see. The thickness of the multitudes of pairs and small groups of warriors, from antiquity to current day, fill the horizon in a perfect circle. Native Americans wear war paint and have bows drawn. World War II marines have purple hearts and pistols. Ancient Vikings, Romans, Mongols, African tribesmen, and the mighty eras of every nation are collected in the armor of their day. The black and white vision ends each time, when I look up and see a 30 foot tall half of a face of a man with dark clouds and fire behind him. He's in big neon colors. His piercing eyes are delighting in the pandemonium and then he fixes his sights on me flying by myself above the mess. The fright wakes me each time. It feels like I meet the essence of evil face-to-face. I've had this vision all of my life.

This dream was worse now. I had identified the 30 foot face. The face was projected to a movie screen in a theater. The American Dream theme of my life purpose was coming to pass. I still didn't know what my part was in the script, but the other actors were heading on stage, one by one, and making themselves known.

I tried to sleep. The images of the dream morphed into a ballet. The stage had white smoke billowing beneath the feet of the dancers in costumes playing out my nightmare. The arts version of ferocious fear was lighter, yet the underlying message was heavy as an anchor on a freighter. A spiritual war of the ages was brewing and I was being shown the premonitions.

# CHAPTER 44
# CHAIN REACTION PARIS

Captain Ed made the crossing to the Bahamas in Blue Daze. Owen went dark again. The Fujitive was absent. Ann was staying in the guest house and looking at condos in West Palm Beach. Ted and I were back in Europe. I was excited because of the directive from Y to travel with Ted. This is what I was supposed to be doing at this time. My life was magical.

In Paris, the coo-coo clock chimed eight bells in Epicure. Ted jumped up and gave a honey and coffee flavored quick kiss from his croissant and cappuccino. Our petit dejeuner ended abruptly as he darted across the lobby towards the Peugeot sedan sent to pick him up for his late morning meeting.

I stayed at the white linen draped table with a spread of fresh fruit salad topped with sprinklings of 18 karat gold flakes and a white chocolate sliver with the Le Bristol logo imprinted on it. The fresh squeezed apple and orange juices were beginning to settle pulp at the bottom of the crystal glasses. The Cristolfe silverware sparkled sprays of light across the white china designed with delicate flowers and butterflies. The voluminous windows trimmed in rich tapestry drapes framed an obsessively manicured garden. A gardener plucked a brown leaf from a blooming camellia bush floating on a bed of bright yellow puffs of petals.

The three-star Michelin restaurant entertained the local dignitaries from the British and U.S. embassies and the Elysees Palace, all a block away. Global tourists were starting celebratory events with champagne. I was set for a shopping day down the tony rue de Faubourg Saint-Honore, from Le Bristol to the Grand Palais at Champs-Elysees. The day prior, I followed the hotel's side street rue Montiagne past the Champs-Elysees to the Golden Triangle closer to the Arc de Triomphe and the Eifel Tower.

I freshened up in our hotel room and took a photo of the panorama from the balcony showing the top half of the Eifel Tower. Ted had photographed me there the prior evening with the twinkling city lights.

Counting my blessings and feeling grateful, I said aloud, "Some days I am happier than others. It seems in joyous times, I am either accomplishing much or quite nothing much at all."

Today was a day to myself to relax and be a pampered Parisian.

I bid "bon jour" to the formal doormen unloading ten Louis Vuitton bags for a petite brunette, wearing ostrich boots with skinny jeans and a tight lilac cashmere turtleneck. Her Pomeranian pooch had a rhinestone collar that matched her sweater. The puppy pranced on his leash like the ponies of dressage in Wellington in Florida.

The gently curving streets looked much like many of the streets in the 8th arrondissement; five stories of monochromatic crème and tan buildings, with first floors of designer shops alternating with the cafes where the shoppers sip espresso and smoke cigarettes. Attendants draped in black coats with top hats and white gloves stood attentive outside the luxury hotels every meter or so, greeting, "bon jour Madame."

Twenty minutes into my trek along the uneven tiled sidewalk, I took a nostalgic stroll around Place Vendome. The Ritz was still under renovation. I had several joyous encounters at the Hemingway bar at the Ritz. I'm normally drawn to the house of Chanel. I'm not a fashionista. I have surf-chick sensibility with a classic wardrobe. I like pearls. I like Chanel because of iconic Coco with her independence and creativity. She empowered women with necessary style changes of her time. I admired successful feminine leaders.

Van Cleef and Arpels caught my fancy this trip as another Parisian icon of indulgence. I rang the bell and the security man gave me entrée to the inner sanctum of the newly renovated art nouveau interior by designer Patrick Jouin. An English-speaking French woman gave me a tour of the museum floor above outlining the 100 year history of the brand. As a brand freak, I savored the detail of the sales seduction.

I chose a simple four-leaf clover luck pendant in mother-of-pearl. I wished Ted best of luck in his meetings as I made my quick decision for the least costly trinket. It still totaled nearly $2500, which the salesperson cleverly advised me was a good deal with the exchange rate and the difference of the cost of making the purchase on Worth Avenue back in Palm Beach. Once you sat down, and your beverage was served, and the associates started buzzing around bringing pieces especially chosen for you, it would be hard to leave without a shopping bag. You were sitting at VC&A ground zero at Place Vendome and you were keenly aware why they were a major international luxury brand, one word, marketing.

As the salesperson wrote up the order at the desk in the cozy beige cocoon of a space, ten alternating attendants and security guards all sibling-looking of similar slim physique and slight stature, with white skin, brown straight hair, brown eyes, all stood erect staring at the glass door. They were eerily quiet and attentive to the pedestrian traffic outside. It felt like an audition for the "City of Angels" film where the angels all stand on the beach in silence and watch sunrise. The salesperson chuckled discreetly as I made this observation. In their employee handbook, it must encourage them to be somber and not giggle. Nobody was laughing.

I took my booty in my white bag as to not draw attention, tucked it in my Chanel black shopper bag, and continued the circular stroll of Vogue magazine popping to life. I shopped the windows of Chanel, Dior, Huebot, Rolex, Jaeger-Le Couture, Lorenz, Baumer, Dubail, Cartier, Louis Vuitton, Boucheron, and Piaget. The Ministrie de la Justice protected by uniformed military with machine guns, clashed with the decadence of my orbit of opulence.

I continued back on Saint-Honoree towards Café Marley at the Lourve plaza. Two blocks away, I took a right on Place de Pyramides, to photograph the Joan of Arc or Jeanne d'Arc statue in the median of the road at the Hotel Regina. I snapped selfies of the golden maiden each visit as inspiration in the honor of feminine heroism and courage based on spirituality.

As I grinned and clicked my lens, my persona transformed from confident American businesswoman, to vulnerable tourist. The melodic French sing-songy voices now ballooned into waves of seven or eight simultaneous languages. I had left the 8th and was now in the 1st arrondissement. The energy shifted almost immediately along Rue de Rivoli with bustling souvenir shops on the left, four lanes of traffic and Tuileries Gardens on the right.

I reminisced for a moment of Kiss Day I planned for Ted the last Paris trip. We visited "The Kiss" marble statue at the Rodin Museum, then got applause from enthusiastic onlookers for our French kiss session in the Tuileries Gardens.

My past memory clicked off as I felt a yank on my purse. I had my passport, tons of cash, and my new good luck necklace in the bag. I had an iron fist on the handles. I glanced at the tugged purse in my right hand. All was still intact except a dangling handle. I stopped in the human stream and it was like when you hook a large pelagic and stop the boat to reel him in and the current shifts to ebb around you.

In that split second, my periphery caught to the left of me to a chest high, round bodied, dark skin, weathered 60-ish woman draped in loose layers of cotton skirts, and long stringy black and gray hair. A large black bag with long handles draped over her shoulder. The canvas decoy sat flat and presumably empty, perfect in size to slide snatched purses right into hers to conceal for a quick getaway. Her black soulless eyes darted back and forth maniacally to my diamond necklace and my bag. She shifted her weight from side to side as her nimble hands floated in front of her like a boxer. In just the space of seconds, my inner warrior was called into being. My father was a Golden Gloves boxing champion so even as a girl, I had lessons in self-protection. I took a deep breath and my chest rose. I peered deep into her caverned wrinkled face into the tiny beady circles of her inner emptiness. Her eyes caught my peer. She jumped back and she gasped. She stood frozen without breathing. By the end of that split second, she turned and sprinted through the sea of black coats and scarves, her tangled gray locks disappearing as though she had not really even been in my presence. The scene was surreal as all the passers-by saw and did not one thing.

I gathered my composure so as not to look vulnerable and attract another of the gypsy gang. Logic told me that she would have a spotter or a manager of some sort watching the fiasco failed purse snatching. I assumed they followed me from Place Vendome. I left the safety of the machine gun bearing guards back in the circle. I walked into one of the tourist shops and realized she had tugged so hard that she had broken the metal ring holding the metal chain of the metal hardware on the bag. She pulled hard. I held harder. You hold tightly to the things you value.

My chain reaction stopped what would have been a catastrophic crime. First of all, I held tightly to what was important to me as I navigated through the busy street. When faced with crime, my reaction was not fear but self-protection and retaliation. If she had stood there another split second my clenched fist could have been in motion. I thanked God that she ran so my Paris memory would not be, "the time you took out the purse snatcher."

I bought 95 Euro nondescript blue purse. A fashion label equals target. Blending was becoming the new normal of blah. Like the fashion industry introduced thin t-shirts and ill-fitting ripped jeans and sold them to affluent teens as trendy. I was still a Chanel girl, but I just needed to be discreet until I felt safe again.

A procession of a dozen sirening police cars startled me as they prodded oncoming cars and scooters dangerously close to the pedestrian sidewalk stream. I wished I had caught her, which was nearly impossible as I was caught off guard. I wished her band of petty criminals were crammed inside the back seats of the speeding police vehicles. I visualized her in hand cuffs getting caught. I would wear my necklace. She would wear metal bracelets of a handcuff variety.

At dinner I shared with Ted the encounter with the thief.

"You know, my instinct is to protect. When the kids were little and in baby seats in the back of my Volvo station wagon, I forgot something at the house so circled back and pulled into my driveway. A young woman was opening my gate to my back yard calling a dog. There was no dog. I had heard on the TV news that morning that the Gypsy Jewel Thieves were making their annual hits in Central Florida. They were using lost dogs as cover. I told her to get off my property and I started chasing her. The kids were locked in baby seats in the car. I chased her all the way down the block till she got in a getaway sedan full of gypsies and they all sped off," I told him.

"That doesn't surprise me that you would chase them," laughed Ted.

"My husband was mortified. Anyway, the police came to write up the report and I could hear on the police monitor that they had just hit two other Winter Park neighborhoods and the police were saying, 'They're baaaakkkkkk...' So, if more people chased them down the street, maybe more streets would be off limits, and they would target another community, or find another way to survive, or shift something somehow," I said.

"One encounter, or two in your case, can't change a culture molded by centuries," Ted shrugged.

"One encounter times three million people Central Florida, or however many people in whatever geographic area, would sure change behaviors, if everyone unified," I suggested.

There was an eerie feeling hovering over Europe with the increasing travel security risks. Random violence ran in headlines more frequently. Tourists were noticeably missing. Our concierge got us reservations effortlessly at all of our favorite Parisian restaurants. We had five romantic once-in-a-lifetime days of touring and then dining at Laurent, Lassere, Tallievent, Drouant, and Epicure near where we were staying at Le Bristol.

We shared our dreams often and would interpret them together. On the fourth day, I shared, "I had this terrible dream. I'm awake now very upset with you. It was very real. In the condo I'm thinking about buying in Palm Beach, I came home and surprised you and you had a big party going on, an orgy really. There were young women, really young like college age running around in the pool, none wearing tops, everyone drunk and disorderly, and you were front and center. It was your party in my place and I decided not to buy the condo for that reason."

Ted responded in shock and disbelief, "You won't believe this. I just had the same dream. You are describing the same party scene. In my case, Captain Ed invited people to my house and it was like a scene from 'The Wolf of Wallstreet.'"

"That is quite coincidental," I said and inside thought, "not." Ted liked his dream. I tuned into it. We were connected.

Then "click" and Ted and I were a little off, like American appliances run on 110 volts, while European appliances are 220 volts. He announced after breakfast he had to get back to The States. I reluctantly stayed solo for the rest of the week in Paris.

I didn't want to stay and I begged him, "I'll change my flight and go back with you."

"You often go before or stay after me all over the world. Why are you acting clingy? This is so not like you. You love Paris. You are already here. Stay and have fun," he insisted.

"I'm having dreams, premonitions, I don't want to travel by myself right now," I admitted.

"Well, you are watching too much TV news. This is crazy. This isn't you talking at all. It's like when we encountered the sharks in the Bahamas. What do you do? You don't stay in the boat. You motor to the next reef and you jump right in to get your confidence back. I'm throwing you back in the water. I don't usually dictate your life but this is what is best for you. You will stay. You will be fine," he spoke with directness like a father to a child.

I would be alone again but there were positives to staying. I focused on the positives that I could visit galleries and museums. I liked art. Oui.

# CHAPTER 45
# THE BELLE AND THE BELL

Ted left. The next day the splashing rain and the gypsy encounter made pedestrian adventures unappealing. I pulled up my laptop and put "Paris" in the document search field. It pulled up my journal notes from 2012. Rarely do spiritual messages make sense in isolation, but the aggregate of affirmations can help me make sense of the world around me and my little world.

I clicked open the Word doc and started reading my journal notes from Nov. 19, 2012, which read:

Y told me, "I am not preparing you for a war of the flesh, but of a war of the spirit. You have been prepared for this.'"

That was in the morning. Later that day, spirituality came to life and flew around the room.

"11/19/12 Mon. 20:58" was marked in the digital camera on the photo I snapped after I recovered from the startle of the clanking, ringing and smashing of the falling bell unto the hardwood floor.

I was setting up my Pinterest account to promote my books. I set up a board and was learning how to import pins on the board. I choose my first five sample sites to populate my board, and surfed around the art site on the religion board. Every board I went to had a bright blue graphic with yellow letters that read, "I'm not afraid, I was born for this." I found it compelling that just that morning, I heard Y's message and now so many people pinned this message.

I found a graphic of Joan of Arc with a rainbow halo-ing over her head and shoulders. Joan of Arc and rainbows were two topics of interest to me, and my writings. Perfect for my new book board, so I read the how-to instructions and pinned the art to my "Marlins Cry" book board.

BAM! It was upon that very instant that the six inch metal bell hurled itself off of the shelf of travel books. Alarm!

The bell settled into four pieces and fell silent. Except for my beating heart and heavy breath, the house was silent again. The computers whirred behind me as I snapped the photos.

I made note of the placement of where the bell had been on the shelf. It was in front of a stack of travel books from five continents I had visited. The small Rome book is the book that actually fell to tip the bell. I was in Rome on 9/11. Was a catastrophe to hit Paris?

I turned on the camera and made note of the placement of the individual parts. If the bell was a clock, and the handle was the center, the time would be 11:11. I held up a photo of the scattered bell parts over a map I unfolded of Paris. If the bell pointed north, the left ornament pointed to the Eiffel Tower and the right ornament pointed to the Arc de Triomphe. In the study of numbers, 1111 is the highest vibration, which I notice and why the pattern was familiar to me. My intuition told me to pull out the map.

I made a quick prayer to Y asking the meaning. I barely spoke enough French to get directions or order a meal. I'm not sure I would be prepared for anything that required too much communication in Paris.

Y responded with great comfort, "The language of the spirit is universal and is translated within each soul."

I had picked up the bell as a souvenir on a trip to Paris the year prior. I had just indulged in reviewing all of my photos and notes from the last Paris trip. On my desk, right by the computer where Pinterest still shined from the monitor, were my favorite of the photos scattered about on top of the bag of momentos and notes from the trip.

Later that afternoon, I went on the Pinterest site on my iPhone and tried to show Ted the "I'm not afraid, I was born for this" graphics. I had never been on Pinterest before this morning. I couldn't find them again. It all was very compelling but quite strange. I didn't use Pinterest after that first day.

Another time, I remembered equally intriguing, a painting fell from the same shelves. The shelves are built-ins so not likely to move at all. I couldn't understand how the ten inch by eight inch canvas oil painting of cows in a pasture could maneuver past Cow Parade collectible breakable art cows to smash on the floor, breaking the frame. I discarded the frame, and placed the cow painting back on the shelf. The two cows once again grazed peacefully on the pink hued canvas. I connected the dots. The painting was by a local artist friend who had gone on an artist sabbatical in France. The painting was of the french countryside.

I pulled out my camera from my purse to research what trip I had been on when I returned to find the painting on the floor. Not just on the floor as gravity would naturally pull an object, but a good three feet from the shelf as if pushed or thrown. Ted was with me when we found the displaced painting. We had been on a trip. I can't recall the date or trip. We had a lot of trips.

The painting didn't fall and the bell didn't bounce. The bell flew as if it was thrown. I was sitting right there and watched the paranormal occurrence. Over the years, the house had a lot of paranormal activity.

Joan of Arc last Paris trip made herself known at the Versailles palace, where a tall white marble statue of her rested among the statues of French male heroes and leaders. That photo was among the stack and reminded me that after I saw the statue, I had a severe sunburn on my neck and chest. That was another week I was in Paris exploring by myself.

Those notes were from 2012, this was now 2016. My note taking didn't help me understand my spiritual purpose, or my romantic relationship issues. My flux and flow it seemed would continue. It seemed somehow Ted, the Eiffel Tower and the Arc de Triomphe had symbolic purpose in my life.

What I was aware of was that the spirit world wanted me to acknowledge Paris. I would pay attention both now and in the future for clues to how that was connected to me and to my life purpose. It could be as simple as a past life.

# CHAPTER 46
# JOAN OF ARC

Another book that was by the Paris bell when it fell was a book I bought at a book-mobile fundraiser at the kids' elementary school. I was immediately drawn to a book on Joan of Arc.

A hint about a past life involving Paris was in the first past life regression I had done with my Christian counselor I used after my divorce. I saw her at some New Age talks at the library after I got divorced so I knew she was open to new concepts in counseling. She suggested my issues with relationships could possibly be from energy from past lives.

I looked up the notes from Sept. 2001, a few days before I left for Sardenia, Italy as 9/11 exploded in The States. She put me under hypnosis. It was my first time. We had a signal that if I moved my finger she would bring me back to full consciousness. The first was a past life with the guy from Naples. We had a happy family and my heart desired to have that same familiar peaceful secure situation. The second was about my life purpose.

My notes from my past life regression on Sept. 6, 2001 read:

She sent me into the next incarnation. In full panoramic view in lifelike realism, I was in this medieval town square with wearing armor. I could feel the metal. I was with the soldiers. The enemies were headed for us to take me away. The townspeople were onlooking with terror. I had red hair. (In real life I started sweating profusely.) I was a young maiden. I knew who I was. I was terrified and safe all at the same time. Determined. Strong. Purposeful. The counselor was encouraging me to look deeper and see more details. I didn't want to go further. My finger couldn't motion because in real life I was frozen in fear. The counselor saw I was distressed and instructed me to go to a different point in this life. In a glimpse, I saw where the men and I were headed, and I didn't want to experience what was before me. I managed to blurt out, "I don't want to be here!" The counselor asked me to note what was making me fearful and brought me out of the hypnosis. We talked about the visions. She said in looking for love, I was simply looking for a family life that I had before, so my heart knew what love was like and desired it in this life. She said also in looking at love, spiritual love, we got my life's purpose; to be obedient and faithful and set an example, to have faith whatever the price.

Intuitively after the session, sitting in the church parking lot, I wrote, "We cannot judge our success in a life by romantic love but rather by the love we give, the love we leave behind for others. Love is not always shared, sometimes it is just given. The rewards are boundless. Love is eternal. All else just fades away. Faith without fear. Be strong."

The suggestion of a link to Joan of Arc was like the connection to Edgar Cayce. I could have been a part of the energy of that saga in that era. More importantly, it gave me reason to explore and educate myself about any possible connections or lessons from those people to this life. Each spiritual experience led me to more insights about who I am in this life. All of history, including our personal pasts, are for learning and growing.

What matters is the moment, of that I was certain.

# CHAPTER 47
# CHAIN REACTION IN FLORIDA

Sunday, June 12, 2016, back in Florida, I was driving from Palm Beach to Winter Park to have lunch with Ted. I hadn't seen him since he left Paris.

I listened with horror to the news talk radio station for three hours as I drove on the Turnpike. The highway was foggy and apocalyptic-like vacant in the early morning hours. I drove in a mental fog as the news poured in. A few hours prior, at 2 a.m., a mass shooting forever changed Orlando.

I called Ted as I drove, "Did you hear about the terrorist attack in Orlando?"

"It was at a gay night club called Pulse. It sounds like a guy drove to Orlando and managed to kill 49 people. Now out of 300 people in the club, why didn't one person have a concealed weapon? It could have been less than 49 losses if there was return fire at the attacker," responded Ted.

I added, "I heard on the radio that over 60 million people visit Orlando each year. Disney is the largest U.S. employer other than the Pentagon. If those 60 million don't show up next year, like the tourists abandoned Paris, the second largest employer, and the whole Orlando market will be in serious strife. This has huge implications."

"Orlando is small town with large population – ruled by a handful. The families from the Wild West days in early Central Florida will take care of protecting their own. Out of all of the 60 million visitors and limitless venues, the shooter hit a gay bar. Notice he didn't try that shit in a country bar," said Ted.

"This is partly about gun control, but wholly about humanity. This rift between the God of Love and the Spirit of Hate is exploding in our communities. It starts in our hearts. There is strength in solidarity. As spiritual people, we are called upon to unite and heal the broken and empower the fearful. It seems impossible, but it's within reach. We have to remind people why the United States was created, for freedom. We have to reconnect the God of Love to the hearts of men," I said.

Ted cut me off, "You spread love. You be the Ambassador of Light. That is what you do. That is fine. I'm going to spray some bullets if those crazies get near me. What we need is for our citizens to take advantage of our Second Amendment rights and arm themselves.

These radicals need to be neutralized. Our military can't do it because it's the smallest and least effective since before World War I. Our leaders are allowing this intolerable violence. Gun control isn't the answer, because the radicals use box cutters, handcrafted bombs, ropes to hang, rocks to stone, or fire, or knives, or speeding trucks, or any number of barbaric methods. Second amendment allows citizens to protect themselves."

I responded, "And the First Amendment gives us the freedom of speech to speak, to share truth, to report. Our era of political correctness and blending cultures has backfired. People are afraid to speak the obvious truths. People don't trust each other. And the media bites on the strategic propaganda designed to divide us."

Ted added, "We are a country of blended cultures. We were designed to do just that. Resilient rebels and fighters settled the U.S. for freedom and look what happens when you give all of humanity freedom. Freedom is an ideal that is not sustainable unless each citizen understands and values the concept of freedom, and is willing to fight for it. This is not a time for sissies."

"I'm getting close to the I-4 exit. Every dollar is a vote. Let's vote for America. Want to meet me at the Four Seasons by Disney? Remember how much you enjoyed the Kobe beef last time we had dinner at Capa," I said.

"Sure. I'll drive to Four Seasons now, I can be there in 45 minutes. I miss you. I need you. I love you. You are my everything. You are my forever. You are my love and my partner and my best friend. I need you now," he strategically changed the subject to romance and love.

He always said that. My ears liked the words. I took the hook like a marlin to a skirted circle hook, "I love you, too."

We met on the patio of Capa on the 16th floor of the Four Seasons. The sky was crying. The harsh wind blew my dress up.

"Looks like hurricane season may come early. Look at this storm rushing in," noted Ted.

"I hope not. After Charlie, I stayed near here at the Ritz. I didn't have electricity for weeks. Then the next few hurricanes hit that year. I lost four oak trees in my yard," I said.

Day became dark before us. The increased foreboding rumbling of thunder sparked a crackling lightning across the horizon. The view was both serene and surreal. A grey cylinder of soaking clouds dripping heavy balls of rain positioned itself halfway between Capa and the dollhouse-size downtown Orlando 30 miles to the northwest.

We were so high that we could easily see for 50 miles in every direction, something not common in flat Florida. The rains marched in goosestep fashion over the carpet of fluffy pine treetops. A sister storm marched towards us from the east.

The staff scurried around covering plastic over the patio furniture around us.

"How is Captain Ed? What did you do?" I asked.

Ted answered under a crash of thunder and I couldn't hear him.

"Who else was there?" I started my normal inquisition.

Again, thunder camouflaged his response but I heard, "Dave something-or-other."

When he lied, it would sometimes lightning even if a storm wasn't around us. We would joke about it.

"I'm not going to test this. I'm going inside," Ted said as he pointed to the sparking sky and spun around towards the double glass doors.

As he spun around, I saw the scene in black and white in slow motion. It looked like a clip from a TV commercial I had produced for a window and door manufacturer. The commercial made the phone ring for the client. People called the store manager to thank him for such a beautiful commercial. The TV viewers said it touched them inside and made them cry. The copy went something like, "X Company Windows and Doors, sometimes for warm hellos ... and sometimes for sad goodbyes."

Then I stopped the questions. I looked at the angry sky. I thought, "God is already angry enough. And his tears are heavy upon this land. His concern is of the wicked, no the wayward wanderers."

Thinking about the energetic chain reaction of one crime against a human in Paris, then a chain reaction of a crime against many humans in Orlando, I sensed as a spiraling Evil Spirit attacking all of humanity. Evil acts undermine Freedom. Fear undermines Freedom.

## CHAPTER 48
## STRAWBERRY MOON SUMMER SOLSTICE

A week after the Pulse attack, on Monday, June 20, 2016, a 70 year lunar cycle yielded a full moon and the Summer Solstice on the same day. The full moon rose as the sun set. The world was in perfect measure of night and day. Sunrise is my favorite time of day and the summer solstice is my favorite day of the year. The sun energy bathed my creative energy.

I posted a photo of me with my broken bag and the abandoned Louvre plaza with the following note on my social media in June 2016:

A Chain Reaction, This Summer Solstice Shine Light & Beauty

The photo is not flattering in any way, to me or to the Louvre in the City of Lights. A random photographer squatted down so I would block the sun. The courtyard was eerily empty as was much of Paris that spring week.

By shops along the Rue de Rivoli, a few blocks away, a gypsy had just attempted to take my bag. She yanked from behind with such force that she snapped the metal chain on the handle. She darted in front of me to try to snatch the purse from the front. Shocked, I stopped and the sea of global tourists shifted pedestrian patterns around us oblivious to the would-be crime. My iron-clad fist held steadfast on the straps. My passport was inside so I had been on high alert. I felt my other fist clench. I stared down at the straggly-gray-haired weathered woman whose eyes darted from my necklace to the purse, shifting her weight like a boxer. My purse, and all of my belongings, were going to peacefully stay in my possession. I felt sorry for her. My energy spoke to her, not my words. Our seconds-long encounter ended abruptly when she looked up at my eyes glaring down into her face. She gasped. She froze. Then the short woman crouched over and darted into the crowd with her empty large black canvas bag, becoming invisible again. Today I picked up the repaired bag back in Florida.

The incident ignited many conversations to be prepared and aware, and to protect oneself with positive energy. The more you practice being mindful, the easier it can become when you need it most.

The Summer Solstice today has the most sunlight of the year. It has the least darkness. From The City of Lights to The City Beautiful, and to humanity worldwide, today is a day to let your Light shine and your Beauty beam. As we focus on Light and Beauty, the healing energy can help transform the dark and the broken.

# CHAPTER 49
# RAINBOWS NEVER LIE

"Is it normal for a rainbow to appear before a storm?" my friend asked as he looked out of my sliding glass doors at dusk.

I fit in a little social time in Winter Park before heading back south.

"It's not normal, but it is noteworthy," I said.

I picked up a pen and scribbled some notes to myself as the summer sun sank and the daily rain started pelting liquid BBs at my windows. I took a photo of the rainbow tucked in the gray skyward fluffs and relaxed into the moment watching my backyard nature theater.

I wrote, "Note to self: The rainbow appears before the storm to assure us that the storm is intentional. The lightning is to startle us and to get our attention. The thunder affirms that danger is present. The wind gusts whisk away that which is no longer healthy or necessary. The heavy downpour pressures the nutrition to the foundation of the roots. After a storm, we expect a rainbow, a promise. A rainbow before a storm is preparing us for a hearty storm, with a spiritual promise for endurance through the passage of an aggressive, egregious or unexpected unpleasant event. The rainbow seekers live under the protection of the painter of the sky. Continue to seek and find."

I wasn't exactly sure for what I should prepare. I sensed it could be for a long term project. I planned for Labor Day weekend to complete a writing project, a book. For every action there is an equal and opposite reaction. In creating messages for Good, the opposite would typically try to thwart my efforts. Whatever was brewing would certainly be tilted in my favor karmically. Rainbows never lie.

# CHAPTER 50
## SYMBIOTIC STING PATROL

Back again in Palm Beach, the word "Hope" that was carved into the railing on the weathered wood stairs at the last south access to the public beach on Palm Beach island was gone. The railing had been replaced with fresh bright wood. The message was gone but the meaning lived on in my mind. Words have power even when removed.

It was a crisp morning with crystal clear waters. I put on a wetsuit top to help if I got near the jellyfish. With plastic outweighing sea life in the oceans, the sea turtles are dying from ingesting plastic. Sea turtles eat their weight each day in jellyfish and if turtles aren't around, the jellyfish prosper disproportionately. Plastic can look like jellyfish to turtles, so they mistakenly eat trash and die. I spent a half hour picking up trash and disposed of it before my swim. Each person each day on the planet can make a difference in many ways.

One time I smacked a startled barracuda in the head hiding in the seaweed close to shore, so after that, I swam a little further away from the shore. I swished out to 20 feet offshore, still close to the beach, and swam perpendicular dodging pink and purple jellyfish. I felt a presence behind me, and stopped and stood up in the 4 foot deep water. I didn't see a predator. I did see a young woman with wide shoulders and narrow hips in a blue one piece. She didn't wear a mask. She stopped, too.

"I'm so glad you are not a shark! I felt something my size shadowing me," I exclaimed.

"I've been a swimmer all of my life. I'm not familiar with these waters, so I followed your guidance. You set a comfortable pace for me. I haven't been in the ocean since a health issue several years ago. I had an unexpected unexplained heart attack at a young age. I almost died. I actually did and came back to life. I didn't have a near death experience but a real death experience, white light and flashing memories and all, just like people describe death," the stranger explained.

"Welcome back to the water! The salt water is healing with positive ions. So, I help heal you and your mending heart with safety in our swimming journey. And you, in turn, heal me. For I am fearful of what I cannot see behind me. But you instead remind me that we lead and encourage and motivate and heal when we least expect it.

It's a wonderful symbiotic healing swim," I said and we went back to freestyle.

After the swim, I hopped on my beach bike and pedaled down the bike path by the intercoastal. I stopped at the dock at the end of North Ocean Avenue. Some baby-faced pre-teen toe heads were fishing from the dock.

"Don't kill him," one said as his friend scraped a knife across a live bait fish on the hook of his rod.

"No, I want him to wiggle still but I want him to bleed so he'll attract a bite," said the other fisherman as he reached in the bucket and gave an unnecessary squeeze to several other live bait fish.

I grimaced at the sight. The jellyfish didn't sting me earlier. I floated with them in their watery world at peace. This visual stung my senses. Somehow, I was overcome with a sense of unnecessary turmoil in the water of a greater magnitude than this dock scene.

The dock faces across the Lake Worth inlet to Singer Island. There was a clamor on the docks and the fishermen and tourists were gathered. A boat must have brought in a trophy fish again.

# CHAPTER 51
## ONE DIES AND ANOTHER SPIES

Ann was on a date with Armando's dad, the new Mr. Right. J didn't answer his phone. I wandered out for dinner. Ted called. I was waiting to get a seat at Bricktops. I took the phone to the ladies' room so I could hear him better. The noise was worse in there with Elvis Presley crooning "Suspicious minds ... asking where I've been ..." Ted called from Nashville or NashVegas as he calls it. He was at Tootsies on Broadway where Patsy Cline moaned in the background, "crazy for lo-ovivg you...." Between the two country music stars, we couldn't hear so he said he would call back.

I walked a block down South County Road to Buccan.

Right as I walked in, a chatty man grabbed my forearm and asked me if I would like a drink. He elbowed me to the far corner of the L-shaped gray marble bar behind a couple perched on the wood bar stools. The stretched leather seat made the man sink and he appeared shorter than he already was. My new friend ordered drinks and handed me one.

"I have to tell you the truth. I'm a retired 20 year Federal Marshall. I'm a private eye now. I'm taking photos of this cheating attorney with this 25-year-old. It's his third date today. He's already got a wife and a girlfriend. Florida is a no-fault state for divorces but documenting cheating does help with mediation. I'm taking photos for the wife. I get paid big money to come to sleek places like this and drink. Before I was in the 'hood hoping not to get killed hunting dangerous fugitives. These guys are easy to tail. I've followed him all week. I just change my shirt but he hasn't noticed me. He's oblivious. I've got two people outside ready to back me up if he does notice me. Business is good. There are a lot of guys like this one in South Florida," he rambled in a hushed tone.

"So, if the subject does notice, I'm between you two and at risk! Thanks for the drink, but I'm not sticking around for this," I said.

I walked back by the attendant of the maze of unisex bathrooms and peeked in Imoto Sushi next door. The popular restaurant was bustling also, so no seats there either, so I left through the valet area. Restaurant hopping was common as the island restaurants were all small with limited seating. Many single people venture out to dinner solo so it's not uncomfortable to do so in Palm Beach. In Winter Park, I would be much less likely to dine by myself. The community culture in the more touristy place makes it more comfortable.

I drove to The Grill. At least there if you had to wait, there was a social place to mingle. I would know other locals. The head bartender at The Palm Beach Grill greeted me with a glass of Stags Leap Chardonnay handed over the dining guests at the bar.

"One today Charlotte?" she asked.

I nodded across the noisy clamor of chatter and leaned against the half wall behind the bar seating area, separating the dining room. There was a two hour wait as usual. Waiting was half the activity of dining there. In the tables, I recognized a famous singer and an author. I realized I was truly a Pi-lander after all these years, when after only ten minutes, she yelled, "Charlotte!" and pointed to a fresh set of white linens and silver placed at a single seat at the bar. I ordered Dover sole and kale salad and went back to people watching. I didn't feel very talkative. A friendly acquaintance kept me company with light conversation.

My phone rang. I assumed it was Ted. I jumped up and ran to the back outside courtyard to talk. We were supposed to leave for St. Barths and had not made flight plans. I looked and the caller I.D. said Captain Ed.

"Hey Cat, I'm here having a beer with J and he's all over me to call you. I was fishin' with buddies and a bunch of boats were circling here outside Sailfish Marina by the bridge. Riviera Beach on the other side of Singer Island is the murder capital of the world, as you likely know. Those idiots throw the bodies off the bridge all the time. Well, someone got to your Fugitive dude earlier today. That creep has been lurking around here this week. He's up to no good I tell you. I took a photo for you but it's blurry. I was pretty far away. I can tell it's him. I got a good look at him since he spent so much time on that orange picnic table next to Blue Daze in Port Lucaya. They said he had a laptop in a plastic bag strapped to his chest. That's what your boy J here is making me call to tell you," said Captain Ed.

"That must be the commotion I saw at Sailfish Marina from the North End dock today. Who is he? How did he die?" I asked.

"I don't know. Us captains and dockmasters were trying to find out who he was for the last few years. He was a weird guy. He was The Fujitive, that's all," said Ed.

"Try to find out anything you can and tell J or call me back," I urged.

Like the Costa Rican tarantula, The Fugitive I had decided meant no harm to me. I decided he was just crazy. That would be easier to deal with mentally than to try to figure out what he was really trying to do. I had been mindfully thinking this way for weeks and weeks, just erasing him from my mind. If I had really believed he was a threat, I would have involved Ted more and alerted authorities.

Secrets sometimes are secrets for valid reasons. I was not meant to know of his secret. The keeper of the secret was now silent. I put it in my past. As for what he was trying to tell me, it was not meant to be shared. Things are always as they should be. Maybe his information was inaccurate. As many truths there are in the world, there are equally as many lies. The world is in balance.

I actually felt relief. I felt spared because knowledge is power, and with power is responsibility. I remembered my lawyer friend's advice, "A wise man once said nothing." Well, the same is being wise to not listen. Why should I get information about my ancestral past in such subversive manner? If there was something my family wanted me to know, they would have told me.

On another note, I was overcome with guilt. I am acutely aware that thoughts and words are powerful. How many times did I wish The Fugitive would flush out of my life? I didn't mean to cause harm to him. I didn't mean for him to die. I just wanted him to leave me alone.

"Please give me peace about this situation," I whispered to Y.

I went back in and dropped some cash on the counter. Outside I sat on a bench in the Royal Poinciana courtyard and Googled the drowning. I looked online. No police report. A mysterious man died who never lived. He was a John Doe. An invisible John Doe. He didn't even get one mention online. Not one police report even as a John Doe. Not even one photo was posted even with crowd watching his body be removed near the marina earlier in the day.

My impending meltdown fueled by action and reaction was about to reach an atomic reactor scale.

An e-mail came in. It was from Ted. It had my name in the subject line but it wasn't intended for me. It was supposed to go to Molly who had been my spiritual advisor for most of the duration of my relationship with Ted. She was an older woman who had become a confidant more than an advisor. She often took up for Ted and assured me he wasn't seeing other women romantically. She insisted each time I asked that he was flirtatious with the women surrounding him, and that they were after him, but he wasn't acting on temptations. He wrote in his e-mail, "Tell her to go to St. B. I'm witttth Dave and Rick in Nish. Shhh. $ Monday."

He must have been drinking, well, of course he was by this time of day in NashVegas. He wouldn't normally have typos. So, he was with Dave which was backwards for Eva, the total bitch Eva.

I felt a shit-storm ass-whipping of words brewing inside of me.

I never considered her to be a romantic rival. Captain Ed called her "The Golddigger." In her own words, when she was trying to inflict pain on me, she bellowed at L'Avenue in Paris to be sure I would hear, "I'm not a wife or a girlfriend, but I get all of these great trips."

She showed an amazing lack of self-respect. She was wrong though, she did have a title, it wasn't girlfriend, or fiancee, or wife, or soulmate, or love of life, but Golddigger. On another occasion, in my darkest hour of 2013, she again made her sordid self known to me and in a restaurant where I was minding my own business and shouted with her lowclass self, "Yes I was there! It was me in Paris and New York and Bahamas and the Beach!"

I didn't know her. The only reason I knew she existed is Ted's odd behavior at times, Captain Ed's slip, Molly's tips, and then she made sure I knew she was lurking in the sidelines. I'm not sure at all if I would recognize her if she wasn't drawing attention to herself. She was rather plain.

I consciously tried to control my emotions. Donna told me I was like the Princess and the Pea where I focused too much on where it hurts. It did hurt. Where I had for too long held my words, they were not to be silenced. Charm could not calm these wild waters.

I heard Y, "Put down your pen."

That meant put down my mental sharp sword.

I stopped digging up the details that had been forgotten for years.

Y said, "I have gone before you to make a safe passage. Your enemies will fall before you."

So, the God of The Universe had the situation under control through karma.

Through her own admission, she had an insignificant title in all of our lives. Now she had a new title, Enemy.

I noted another alarming fact. Enemies was plural.

Her dispicable insignificant presence might be denied or overlooked or wrangled out of by the boyfriend somehow but now we had a bigger problem. Ted was controlling my confidant and advisor. He always said that money talks. His money was now talking to my advisor and telling her what to tell me! I was shocked. I was pissed. It was bad enough that "Teddy Bear" had the bimbo brigade following him around but now this betrayal from a woman I would have never ever suspected.

Then an even bigger emotional eruption burst. Rick was the cyber stalker. What? Ted had invested in a company of that evil sorcerer so they knew of each other. Now they were socializing together behind my back? This simply could not be true.

I had suspected for some time that Ted might be accessing my computer and e-mails. I had deduced it was arranged by the I.T. guy Don that helped out with forensics on my phone and computers in 2011. He likely justified spying on me in 2011 as a way to protect me. I had safety concerns of a physcial nature as well as cyber at that time. We didn't know how crazy the stalker was. Well, this new twist could certainly explain how Ted found someone to teach him how to do such a vile thing as cyber spying. Even if he could explain this away as not the Rick of cyber crimes was not in Nashville but another Rick, Ted was in my computer spying on me. It was undeniable. While the volcano was erupting, this lava spew was going to burst, too. Let's start with, I was supposed to arrange an island getaway. I had not yet told him it was St. Barths, that detail was however in my computer and phone. He told Molly in the e-mail St. B, but I had not yet told him. That was a on a long list of undeniable iron-clad clues of cyber spying.

Then a text dinged, "Cat, I can't make it to St. B. You go. Get a flight and let's talk tomorrow. I'll try to come later in the week but not looking good for that. Love, Ted."

He was so duplicitous. I tried calling. I wanted to know for sure if he sent the e-mail. Maybe the e-mail was orchestrated by a cyber stalker. Worse things than that happened during the cyber stalking bouts. Maybe he wasn't with either of my two nemeses. If he was, he hurt me in the two places that I would be most damaged, by cheating on me and by cyber spying on me.

Ted didn't norally slip on details. Maybe he was taking drugs with his new marijuana investment peers. Maybe he wanted me to know. Maybe he was pulling the rubber band for a grand snap. Ka-pow was now.

# CHAPTER 52
## LOVE NEVER DIES

Ann came back to the guest house after a date with Armando's dad Mr. Right. I was packing for St. Barths.

"What's that smell?" she asked.

"I lit some aromatherapy sage to clear the space energetically," I responded.

"Well, if your goal is to clear men out, it should do the trick," she complained lightly.

I gave her the highlights of my saga and added, "You can't change people. They have to change themselves. Ted likes his lifestyle. I have to change how I think about him."

"So, I'm confused. How do you think about him?" she asked skeptically.

"Well, I am completely heartbroken. As hard as I try to not commit, he has my heart. Someone advised me that you keep people in your life until it hurts more to stay than it would hurt to walk away. I'm going to walk away for a while, likely not forever. I am accepting him for who he is, and allowing him to be that person. I am not ending the relationship. I am redefining it. Love never ends. I cannot stop love. I will complete my karmic promise to be with him until the ends of his days in this life. That does mean we live in a committed relationship. I will be with him in love as his forever friend. I am here in this life to fulfill my spiritual obligation and then say goodbye to him. Otherwise, he will show back up in my next life," I said.

"That sounds more like something an enabler would say in a co-dependent role. You don't make sense to me about men," said Ann who was religious and attended church regularly but didn't have a grasp of or even an interest in personal spirituality.

"I admit I did become more attached to him after the stalkings. Fear and trauma shift our thinking and our behaviors, sometimes until we heal and sometimes forever. I was so vulnerable and weakened after that ordeal. Love don't always make sense. Just as importantly, I have to be who I am to be. I pray about a man and God answers me about mankind. I have to honor what I am feeling now. I have to free up my time to first understand my life's work, and then to do my life's work," I added.

Then I added something Ann would understand, "High roller dating is fun until they steam roll over you. It was a struggle after so many years to be the best catch in the room to keep his attention. I had his heart, but not his full attention. I need and deserve more."

I switched topics to my work so Ann wouldn't harp on Ted. You can't un-ring a bell. The bell was ringing and ringing and ringing.

I asked Ann about her date. That effectively took the conversation to her and her new beau. He was the one. She would be with him forever. She always said that.

## CHAPTER 53
## SOUTHERN GENTLEMEN IN SAINT BARTHS

In a small charter plane with one couple and a pilot, I dropped from the sky over the small mountain to the short runway and the plane screamed to a stop just before it splashed into the ocean. It was so much more fun when I had Ted with me to laugh about it. Life was more fun with Ted. I kept consciously trying to shift my thoughts to happiness of me not we. I settled in to The De Haenen suite at Eden Rock St. Barths. I poured a glass of the complimentary French champagne and stepped on the wrap around balcony with panoramic views across the turquoise Bay of St. Jean where just a few months ago, I sat with Ted.

I did what I always did when I was uneasy. I wrote as art therapy. I took a pen and a legal pad to a comfy chaise lounge and penned my first thoughts.

The pen wrote, "Why I like Southern Gentlemen immediately: Manners. They stand when I leave and return to a dinner table. They might call it supper. Their mamas taught them etiquette. Mama. She gets a mention in the first few minutes, along with much of the family tree. Loyal. If they are married, 'my wife' gets a mention in the first few exchanges. Heritage. They are proud of their southern hometowns. Friends. They tell a funny story from their early childhood. You get the feeling they've been laughing with their buddies for a lifetime. A friend from kindergarten might call while he's telling the story about him. Nicknames. My name is ___. But people call me ___. Genuine. In a world of superficiality, they stand out. In the first few minutes, you know a lot about them. And they ask a lot of questions of you. They are genuinely interested in your answers. Smiles. From across a room you can see the Southern charm spread through the smiles of the people talking to Southern gentlemen."

I gravitate to the cheerful funny Southern types but I was open to destiny. I'd like to have the family God promised on the church pew. I'd like to attract someone of similar vibration. I actually wasn't sure if I was ready to date or if I should put myself back on dating detention for a year as I had done in the past after heartbreaks. If I was going to date, it would only be my placeholder name Harrison Gore or HG. I started with the crossword puzzle clues that might help me bring his energy into my present. Through my soul searching in church, 20 years ago, there was a sermon on David with his defining character of 'meek' or strength under control. I was shown during the sermon that this would be the defining character of HG. Meek was a must for my man.

Through 20 years of readings, I had a pretty good idea of the type of man my twin soul would be. I started making a list, "Age within ten years of mine, brown hair with gray flecks, 3 children, real estate, meet him at a bar with a Paul, his initials are ..." I stopped and put a big "x" on that list. From this point forward, I vowed to listen to guidance given directly within me. I left the word "meek" and drew a heart by it.

Country music was sliding across the flat bay from the world-famous open-air bar Nikki Beach next door. It was 11:11 a.m. I walked along the beach 150 feet to the entrance and took a seat on a wood picnic table in the back by myself to watch the revelry crank up and escape before it got too crazy. The Gold Rush party had an American cowboy theme and everyone was in costume. The servers ran around galloping on toy hobby horses. A fringed mini-skirted server in a pink feathered cowgirl hat came to take my lunch order.

A Marlboro man walked up and said, "Put her lunch on my bill. May I join you? I have some buddies coming. My name is Paul but my friends call me Bubba."

He was hilarious. He mentioned his mother and father and where they settled in the pioneer days, in Nashville just an hour or so from my mother's family in Greeneville, Tennessee. He mentioned his ex-wife. I was pleased he was single. The more he talked, the more I noticed how handsome he was. He started asking all about me but I wasn't up to answering. I had to come up with some answers before I could verbalize them! Besides, on the short sandy stroll over, I decided a few months of dating detention would be beneficial for me. He lived in Florida and we exchanged numbers to meet sometime in the future.

"You know, you have this beautiful rose color around you. Your outer dominant color is blue, true blue. You are loyal to a fault," he said reading my aura.

"Oh boy! I just don't need any more input from the Universe. I'm listening. I'm listening. OK, OK, I'll act," I responsed being animated to bring humor to his wise words.

"I'm a chatterbox," he said as he stood up when I prepared to leave.

"No, charming! Really! You have no idea how valuable you are to my day and what a blessing you are," I said.

I thought how specific the Universe works. I put the first chapter in my "Secrets of the Southern Shells" book titled "Be Careful What You Wish For." Affirmations and manifestations of deeply held desires are more real to me than the sand I was crunching below my flip flops.

If this Paul was meant to be, he couldn't not call me. He would be completely compelled to follow up with me. In the meantime, I was not a hopeless romantic but a hopeful romantic. There was always space for a miracle and Ted would shift to be my forever man. After all, I was the one who shared, "Believe in a Miracle." I never dated the once predicted three men at once. I likely never would. I am a one-man woman. When I give, I give wholly and completely even when perhaps I should not. I can't change who I am. I don't want to change that about me.

With Ted, and other boyfriends, I would patiently wait for them to mold into my twin soul. I would try to be sweet enough and tolerant enough to meet their needs. Ultimately it wouldn't work and I would let go gently like guiding a newborn baby turtle to sea. Many readings said my twin soul was coming back to me. That could be from a past life, but it could also be one of my boyfriends. Many of them were in my Soul Group from past lives, so they were in both categories of then and now. I treated each one with kindness as though I would see them again when it was time for goodbye.

The first order of the day was to be a voice to myself. As a result of trauma and a weakened state, I had grown complacent and comfortable with compromise. All of the recent reminiscing with Ted actually helped to give me closure for this part of our lives. We shared so many precious memories which will remain with me forever. He is undeniably in my Soul Group so he's not out of my life, just being re-defined so we can have a healthy relationship. Maybe that space would be for a time or maybe for the remainder of this life. I wasn't sure. I just knew my broken heart needed space.

My next love story would start with the chapter where I loved myself well. Practice makes perfect, especially with love. I made an affirmation that I would not be silent in matters of the heart. In order to fully heal, and forgive and forget, I first had to feel. In order to do the feel and heal dance, I had to communicate better. I intended to no longer delay heartbreak for happy in the moment. I had a blueprint of self-protection by not letting people get truly close. I spent time with boyfriends but I didn't hold them accountable as much as I should have. I allowed behaviors because I wasn't willing to ask hard questions. I didn't want to hear the answers. I didn't ask and I didn't answer. I knew that, "To know and not to act is not to really know." In that moment, in an effort to no longer need self protection in romantic relationships, I shifted to a pattern of communicating with complete integrity. Everything you think and do everyday is a choice. As a professional communicator, I was excellent at communication in business and with friends. It was in my romantic relationships that I lacked confidence to hold them to Truth. One shift down. That was a big one for me. More to come?

I peeked around the corner from the balcony with the binoculars on the table and Paul's lifelong friends had filled the picnic table. They were all good looking and outwardly chatty and happy. I had an inkling from my former patterns that I should have stayed. But it wasn't "IT" for me. Maybe this was the predicted turning point when Donna said I wouldn't want to be an "IT-girl."

The gravitational pull of the panoramic paradise view held me captive. I slathered on some of the Eden Rock lilac fragranced lotion on my arms and delighted in the relaxing aroma. I poured another glass of the champagne in the crystal champagne flute. I was incredibly grateful for the experience of this moment.

I pulled out my pen to create poetry out of pain. I affirmed, "Pen Over Men."

## CHAPTER 54
## LOOKING THROUGH LENS

All of life is love or lessons. I hoped the lessons would wane.

What I knew is what I didn't know. I had no idea what I planned to do next other than heal physically, mentally, emotionally, and spiritually. At our darkest most heartbreaking times are when we have space to re-create.

Creating is what I needed to do to feel like myself again. Other than ghostwriting, I had postponed writing because I didn't have any answers. Harrison Gore twin soul and my life mission were not yet fully defined. From this point, I decided life was to be lived and not figured out. So, there world!

As I divorced so many years ago, my personal and spiritual explorations were met with stiff resistance from complete apathy paired with just-be-quiet advice or fundamentalist strict thinking around me. Both extremes suffocated me with the same feedback. Just look pretty and be sweet. For this major heartbreak, unlike before, I had permission to explore. I was totally free this time. My children were raised. My clients were waning. My love life was blank. The Pi-landers may or may not notice if I was or was not there. I had been distanced from my longtime friends because of travel and all the bouncing back and forth in Florida, but also because I didn't want a confidant. I wanted to figure things out on my own and have a happy ending to the story. I, once again, had so many blessings, but I just wasn't at peace inside.

All of this Freedom I found a bit intimidating as I sat by myself in the seaside luxury suite. It was a quiet fear like when people win the Lottery and fear that a year later they will be broke. I had other concerns. Not only was I quite alone, but I had enemies. I had no idea who the enemies were or why they considered me a threat in any way.

I didn't want to be empowered. I wanted to first be enlightened.

I had gratitude, karma and forgiveness in full motion. I also felt abundance and I picked up a $20 bill. I visualized a big stack of them, then stacks and stacks of them. Great wealth was never a goal. Supporting myself and my family using my talents and skills was, however, a necessary ongoing goal.

I thought how ironic that "In God We Trust" was on the $20 bill. The misguided had become devoted to the currency itself. It's like our forefathers sent us a hint for future generations molded into the coins and printed on paper bills. I felt we need to bring Trust back to God. Just like renewing wedding vows in a marraige, the society needed to renew comitment to a solid value system. Just like I was re-inventing new patterns for love, by starting with love of self, then love of others, the re-grounding of America could follow the same healing process starting in the hearts of men.

This brought back thoughts of Donna's 2001 prediction about the twisting of the American Dream. The original Dream basically was for individuals to be able to work hard and have freedoms and rights to live as they like with equal opportunites, following laws of course.

I looked up the Declaration of Independence of the 13 Colonies in 1776: "that all men are created equal, that they are endowed by their Creator with certain unalienable Rights, that among these are Life, Liberty and the pursuit of Happiness."

Donna's vision of miscommunication and discord had come to pass. Something I could not imagine in 2001. The American Dream was being battered with negativity. Anti-American mantras hit the news daily shockingly from our own citizens. Disrespect was rampant at every level of society towards any person or entitity of influence or power. People picked sides like sport team rivalry and naievely cheered maniacally and uninformed for any topic to debate. The culture and history were being scrutinized, minimized or discarded. Ironically some high profile citizens who benefited with great wealth and prestige from the American Dream, like some celebrities, politicians and athletes, were among the worst offenders of disrespect of the very freedoms that gave them their fame and fortune.

American Freedom concepts for some had morphed into greed, entitlement, and lack of work ethic. Some is enough to tip the scale. America is based on individual rights so individuals have to share a common value system for self-regulation to sustain the freedom-based honor system.

In part, a lack of knowledge and understanding caused the shift to a culture of disrespect. How can you practice a doctrine if you haven't learned it? In recent generations, the family structure fragmented leaving a home life that lacked traditions, safety, substance and a sense of belonging. The belonging is big in the shift. It left a void inside hearts and homes. History was no longer taught in schools. Colleges were encouraging disrespect. The church as the community hub was undermined by scandals and indifference. Justice for All now transformed into justice for all of those who can pay. Pinocchio politics rewarded lies and a greed-grab for global contacts, personal power, control and excessive personal financial benefit over the protection of the people of America and the core values.

With the cracks in the ethos, the American Dream was in threat of other entities with very different ideals leading America. Citizens could wake up to a nightmare if they didn't wake up during The Dream. Divisiveness equals destruction.

Just like I had shifted to a blank page in my own life, the country had a big pink eraser scratching hard on blank paper. Just what would be the forthcoming words?

I felt, "Unite the leaders. Empower the Americans. Educate the Sheeple. Enlighten the lost. Awaken the souls."

The thoughts felt overwhelming. An individual can't cure society's frailties. I was simply an observer. I had no power to make any shifts. What I could control is my individual soul to raise my own vibration.

I focused on myself and meditated on, "Seek Truth through LENS. Dwell upon that which is L. Lovely, E. Enlightened, N. Noble, S. Serene. LENS." That meditation triggered my mind to remember to see the world through God's LENS. It was my soul's purpose, like a lens, to spread and disperse light through writing.

I wasn't a history buff or involved in politics. I was meek, defined as strength under contol. I was a writer in the background of society. I felt my inner voice, layered with years of soul-searching, encouraging a notion, an idea, a few words. I could do that. If I inspired one person, it might be a person who could make a positive difference for healing.

I practiced the Laws of Attraction and I sensed my intentions would attract the necessary creative people for a project. What I could contribute is to be authentic, be me, be Cat. As a Dreamer, I could be a Cat-alyst.

I would go back to Palm Beach and be a Catalyst for my own personal dreams. I would be a catalyst for The American Dream, too.

Blue ink flowed onto the cotton blue lined paper, "'Raising the Bar, Men and Mankind' written by a Believer in The Dream. Starring Harrison Gore. Screenplay. Scene One."

THE END for now

## OTHER BOOKS BY CASEY TENNYSON

2008 “Lessons from a Falling Leaf” inspired courage to choose change in your life. The small book was created to promote the artists who illustrated the book.

2010 “Secrets of the Southern Shells” captured a Southern mother’s advice through the adventures of starfish Star in a short story. The book was also illustrated by artists.

2012 “Bait for Fish Bigger Than I Am” is a simple short story about catching a marlin. It’s a travelogue for boating and fishing in Abaco, Bahamas.

2012 “Marlins Cry A Phishing Story” The Digital Damnation of Civilized Society cried out an alarm for cyber safety. The novella has 85 tips for cyber safety woven into the story line.
*If you like “Catalyst Palm Beach” you will like this book.*

2015 “Secrets of the Southern Shells” Second Edition gift book captured a Southern mother’s advice through the adventures of starfish Star in a short story. The book was illustrated by the author with photos of Florida and Bahamas coastlines and with drawings by her daughter.

2019 “Catalyst in Palm Beach” ignites Awareness through a tale of travels, trysts, tragedies, universal Truths and the quest for unrequited True Love. The characters from “Marlins Cry A Phishing Story” develop further in this novel.